Dean Knight is a writer from South East England, who has had a passion for story telling since a young age. A fan of action and adventure stories from across films, books and video games, Dean has always wanted to create a deep and immersive world which can capture the reader's imagination and stay with them long after the final page. *The King Chronicles: Arcanum* is his first full length novel and provides a thrilling adventure which will take readers on a hunt for life changing treasure through a weave of both real and fictional history.

Dean Knight

THE KING CHRONICLES: ARCANUM

AUSTIN MACAULEY PUBLISHERS™

LONDON • CAMBRIDGE • NEW YORK • SHARJAH

A CIP catalogue record for this title is available from the British Library.

ISBN 9781398439436 (Paperback)
ISBN 9781398439443 (ePub e-book)

www.austinmacauley.com

First Published 2022
Austin Macauley Publishers Ltd®
1 Canada Square
Canary Wharf
London
E14 5AA

Chapter One

An intense flash of light in the distance broke across the skyline and caught Arthur's gaze, as the dull thud and crackle that followed met his ears a moment later. A series of premature fireworks were dancing amongst the cityscape, and a few people on the train looked out in awe. It was New Year's Eve, and the city of Rome was set to be the usual party capital, with revellers from around the world descending en masse to see in the New Year. He looked away and back down to his book and regained focus on the matter at hand, which was not within the text that filled the page.

Arthur reached into his jacket pocket and discretely took out a small folded piece of paper. He unfolded it and placed it within the book and refreshed himself with the task set. He had taken up a contract from a rather mysterious and elusive individual known only as 'The Collector'. This person had a set of rare diamonds and documents stolen from him a few days prior.

It had been discovered that a meeting between the criminal responsible and an unknown third party was set for this night. Arthur had been tasked with intercepting the thief and taking the stolen items back; however, if he was able to tail him and find out who was behind the theft, The Collector would be most pleased.

Arthur looked down the carriage taking in the faces of whom he could see before looking down at the image that was printed for his eyes only. A rough-looking man with a near buzz cut, stubble and piercing eyes was the target. Arthur looked up again, and half a dozen or so seats down on the opposite side of the carriage was a man who fit the description. The man appeared slightly pressured, often glancing at his watch and fiddling with the briefcase he had on the table in front of him.

Arthur had already checked this out, a black case with the number seven-hundred and twenty engraved along its side in small print. This was a sorting reference that The Collector had given, so Arthur knew this was the one he needed to acquire.

A train announcement soon came through the intercom, advising that the arrival at Roma Termini was a minute or so away. As this was the last stop, people began shuffling around, collecting belongings and standing up. Keeping his eyes on the man, Arthur remained seated as the train came to a stop at the platform. The doors opened, and people began to depart, which temporarily broke his line of sight on the man.

A few tense seconds passed before Arthur saw the man had gotten up, moved through the train doors and started a brisk walk along the platform towards the exit. Arthur took the file out of the book, placed it back in his pocket and left the book on the table. He got up, exited the train and began slowly following the man, maintaining a distance of around ten metres. Soon reaching the end of the platform, they both descended an escalator that led to an area with a range of shops, which was very busy and filled with people dashing about.

On the way down, the man kept looking around and behind, glancing up at Arthur. The men soon got off the escalator, and Arthur kept the same distance behind the target as he made his way through the shops and towards the exit. Turning again, the man saw that Arthur was still directly behind him, whereas other passengers had gone their own ways. He went over to a payphone and dialled a number.

Arthur walked directly past him and headed to a news stand a little further along. He stood pretending to read a newspaper while keeping an eye on the man. The gentleman hung up the phone and resumed walking towards the exit. Arthur followed a moment after, but the target now realised he was being followed.

He began to pick up the pace as an early test of Arthur, who also picked it up. The man looked back and increased speed again before going into a fast run. Arthur, knowing it was now obvious he was following the man, gave chase, and the two moved to a full sprint through the station, with the man in front not so graciously pushing people out of his way.

They ascended the steps and headed into the area directly outside of the station. A few more fireworks illuminated the sky but could not be heard over the hustle and bustle of the area. It was very crowded and using this to his advantage the target ran into the dense concentration of people and pushed a man off a motorbike, revving up and taking off into the street ahead. Arthur, seeing no alternative, took one that was next to the now stolen bike and was hot on his trail. The owner of the bike, who was at a nearby shop, could be heard shouting in angry Italian after Arthur and waving his arms in the air, which Arthur saw in the rear-view mirror and slightly grinned to himself.

The target drove fast along the road as they approached Piazza Della República, where he took a left and accelerated quickly down the Via Nazionale. Arthur was not far behind and glanced at the lit up curved face of the building in front before hitting the accelerator hard and making some distance up. The traffic started to get heavier, and Arthur was forced to weave in and out of it at high speed as he tried to get level with the target. As he got closer, the man turned and fired a handgun several times at Arthur in an attempt to stop him. Arthur drove behind a lorry, blocking the shots before picking up speed and resuming his pursuit.

The chase soon began cutting through footpaths between buildings as the man became more desperate to escape. A gap had opened up between them, but as Arthur left the more claustrophobic area, he sped into the large open space of Piazza Venezia and saw he was still in with a chance of catching him. More fireworks illuminated the sky ahead as he found himself hurtling towards the looming impressive structure of the Museo Nazionale.

With its architecture lit up, it stood out amongst the scenery, and as he rode past, he couldn't help but glance over in awe. The man shot a few more bullets at Arthur, all missing as he was balancing a briefcase in one hand over his wrist while maintaining the bike and firing wildly with the freehand. He then placed the gun back in his jacket and hit the throttle. Arthur began to wonder if this chase wasn't as random in direction as he first thought, as the man was heading towards the River Tiber.

A few streets more and they came out by Ponte Sisto bridge, and the target took an unexpected turn off the road and down a flight of stony steps to the edge of the river. Arthur hit the steps a few seconds later and almost fell off the bike as the steepness and speed caught him off guard. He reached the bottom and saw the man had thrown the bike to the ground and was running towards two speedboats with a small number of armed men.

"We must go, now!" the target shouted as he boarded one of the boats.

"You two, stop him!" he shouted, pointing at Arthur as the boat he boarded took off with speed.

With that, the two men drew silenced assault rifles and began firing at Arthur, who immediately ducked behind a nearby set of crates and various junk. The hail of bullets thudded the other side of the crates, and Arthur knew they would not hold out for long. He drew his handgun, also silenced, and returned fire.

After a series of brief exchanges, he took them down and quickly ran towards the boat and boarded it. He could still see the target fleeing in the other boat in the near distance, so took off in the boat after him. After less than a minute, he had caught up.

"This guy is persistent! I'll drive, take him out," the target ordered the man, who nodded and turned, picking up his assault rifle. Arthur saw this and took evasive action as a hail of bullets came at him. A few hit the side of the boat, but that was as close as they got. The gunfire temporarily stopped, and the man could be seen reloading, so Arthur took his chance, got closer and took a few shots of his own.

The last few hit the man, who fell into the river. This got the attention of the target, and in a panic, they veered the boat off the river towards the nearest landing point, ramming it into the riverbank and fleeing on foot. Hot on his heels, Arthur pulled the boat up alongside and resumed the chase, sprinting as fast as he could. They didn't get far, and as they reached, the underside of the St Angelo Bridge near Castel Sant'Angelo exhaustion set in with the target.

Arthur got right behind him and tackled him to the floor, which caused the man to drop the briefcase. The men began striking each other with forceful punches, and Arthur soon started to dominate. The men got to their feet mid brawl, and after taking a knock-back, the target drew his handgun at Arthur.

"Enough games," he shouted. "Who are you?"

"It doesn't matter who I am," Arthur responded. "What matters is what you stole needs to go back to where it came from. Now hand it over."

"I am afraid that cannot happen. Do you have any idea who ordered this, who I am taking this to?" the man said in a raised tone. "They won't take kindly to a failed delivery, mark my words, they will come looking for you."

"It doesn't matter. I have already been sent for you, and it is coming with me, regardless of who you are working for," replied Arthur.

"The only way you will be taking this is over my dead body, and seeing as though I am the one aiming the gun, you have no chance," the man said smiling through blood-soaked teeth.

"Oh, really," Arthur muttered, as he quickly drew the empty handgun from his jacket and threw it towards the thief.

This caught him off guard, and he dropped his weapon and the briefcase. Arthur took his chance and started punching him again, with the distant pulsing of dance music from the nearby New Year celebrations providing both a rhythm and cover to the scuffle.

After a short second bout, the thief appeared to give in. Arthur stood, picked up the briefcase and loaded gun, and began to walk away from the thief who was slumped against a wall.

"You are a dead man. I promise you that. I will be seeing you again," he shouted as he spat out a little blood. Arthur turned as he said this and saw the man pass out. He looked back and carried on walking, eager to get out of the city before any more attention was drawn to what happened.

He wiped the blood from his face and walked up the stairs and back onto the St Angelo Bridge, getting out his phone and dialling the number that The Collector had told him to call once he had retrieved the requested item. After a few moments, the call connected.

"It is done," said Arthur.

"Come to where we last met, tomorrow evening, and we will reconvene then," The Collector responded.

"Okay, see you there," confirmed Arthur. As soon as the words left his mouth, the phone cut off.

Chapter Two

The opening creak of the old wooden door gave the grandeur of the building the vibes you would expect, of both wonder and character. As Arthur walked into the main study of The Collector, he could see the man himself, facing the window looking out onto the land below. The noise of Arthur's entrance got his attention, and he turned and smiled, raising his hand in welcome. His short grey hair was combed over, and although a short man, he made up for it in charisma and wit.

As per usual, he was smoking a large cigar, something Arthur had come to expect over the years. He was an older gentleman in his sixties, who Arthur had met many years before on his early archaeology expeditions. He had been funded by this man when he was first starting out, and he owed him a lot, no longer in financial standing, but what he felt his career was worth. Although known as The Collector by many in the community, due to his immense wealth enabling a large assortment of treasures to rival a museum, he was named Franklyn Davies to those closest to him.

"Arthur, my friend, it is good to see you again so soon."

"You too."

They walked over to each other and shook hands warmly.

"Still not kicked the habit I see?" Arthur quipped as he smiled at the cigar in Franklyn's mouth.

"After the dangers that I have managed to outlive in this fascinating interest that we have Arthur, this is one that I won't even consider, especially at my age."

"Now that is a fair point, I can't argue with that!"

"Ha, no you cannot. And I see in your possession you have something that belongs to me?"

"I do indeed, right here," Arthur confirmed, holding up the briefcase.

"Please, place it here for me," Franklyn said, gesturing towards his desk, which was unusually clear of clutter. "I want to see if that thicf took anything or tampered with it. Did you take a look inside?"

"No, I checked the serial number and the description and that was it."

"Then come here, my friend. I want you to know what is in it, and why it was so important to me that it got back in one piece as soon as possible. If this did fall into the wrong hands, I fear what may happen if they understood its potential."

Franklyn entered a code and clicked open the briefcase. He slowly opened it, and Arthur saw what was hidden within, a large set of diamonds and a series of documents neatly folded in one corner.

"Wow, they look like they are worth something!" Arthur exclaimed.

"These were something I inherited from my Grandmother, great diamonds that she was gifted by someone she aided in The Great War. They are priceless to me," said Franklyn.

"I can see why you would go to any length to keep them safe, and in your possession, they are beautiful."

"They are indeed. However, that is not why the briefcase was stolen."

"No?"

"Not a chance. The real reason is this," Franklyn said as he picked up one of the small assortment of folded documents.

"You have got to be kidding, what could possibly make those worth more to you than those precious diamonds?" Arthur said, rather perplexed.

"Take a seat. I would like to tell you a brief story, if I may. What lies within this document should really peak your interest."

Arthur nodded, and the two men sat on chairs that were already at the table the briefcase was set out on.

"Have you heard of the Sutandan Empire, which thrived over a thousand years ago in what is now known as Peru?"

"I believe so yes, they were allies of the Mayan Civilisation?"

"Yes, that's right. As history tells it, they were a hugely successful ancient superpower. They aggressively expanded over whatever land they could and were able to control large parts of the southern continent. The King was never satisfied and always wanted more, and they soon discovered an island hundreds of miles away.

"As it was uninhabited, they quickly colonised, and it became a key part of the empire's footing in the west. As it was so far from the main Sutandan city, not everyone who lived there was aware of its existence. The location was forged onto an artefact that became known as the Arcanum Disc, and it was stored deep within its governmental halls."

"So the King expanded his empire but didn't tell all of the island's location? Did they know it existed?" Arthur asked intrigued.

"I believe so. I imagine people back then were so used to living in one place that they really didn't care for where something like that was. Exploring was really left to the higher end of society and the military, so they were quite content."

"That does make sense. I assume that the people who moved to that island were chosen?"

"A mix, as I understand it. Some were, but as stories of an addition to the empire grew, people volunteered. Where was I? Ah yes. Years later, Sutanda was at war with a rising power from the north known as Mahindra. The fighting had been mainly away from the centre of Sutanda, so the war effort wasn't really being felt at its heart.

"The enemy knew this and wanted to strike but was biding time until a weakness was found. During the early battles, some ships were followed to the island, and to the surprise of Mahendran soldiers, they had discovered a lightly defended part of the Sutandan Empire. They decided to attack, and the island was decimated. This gave them a huge confidence boost, and seeing it as a weakening of the enemy, they took the fight to the heart of the Sutandan Empire.

"Soon, the attack was mounted, and the city was quickly brought to its knees. As the assault on the island was unknown to its leaders, in a desperate attempt to save the island and its inhabitants, as well as his empire from completely falling into the hands of his enemy, the King ordered that the Arcanum Disc be split into three pieces and hidden throughout the world. The city soon fell, and the country was destroyed."

"So the Sutandan people just surrendered?" asked Arthur.

"With the army devastated and the monarchy murdered, they had no choice. They did eventually rise up many years later in a civil war and overthrow the Mahendran rule, but it took a long time."

"And do we know if, as they were not all aware of where it was, the people ever found the island again?"

"The story of the island and the war that focused around it was recorded in various scribes and tales and filtered through the centuries. Over the years that followed, both the Mahendran's and the people who rebuilt Sutanda aware of its existence attempted to relocate the island many times but never found it again. The final fate of the island is officially unknown, but many believe it was washed away by the oceans in raging storms and tsunamis."

"That is quite the story, genuinely fascinating," said Arthur. "But what does it have to do with the documents in front of us?"

"I too have spent many years of my life looking for this place. I can feel the desire that people over the centuries have had for its discovery. If the riches of Sutandan treasure, civilisation and architecture are out there still waiting to be found, then I want to be able to bring it back to the world."

"And these documents are what, a map?"

"Not quite. As told, to discover the island, you first need the three Arcanum Disc pieces, which according to legend will reveal where it is when put together."

Arthur stood up shaking his head. "So you're telling me to find the one needle in a haystack, you need to first find three that are smaller still? It sounds quite impossible to me."

"Now that's what I initially thought, however, after years of study, I feel I have hypothesised the most likely location for the first piece."

Franklyn pointed at a map with the coordinates he had jotted down in marker pen on the document in front of him.

"I believe this is where a search should take place," Franklyn said with confidence.

"The Caribbean Sea?"

"Yes. Nearby the main part of the Mayan Civilisation, there is a stretch of small islands, and I firmly believe that at least one of the pieces was kept by the Mayans for safekeeping, in return for what I do not know, but documents from the period speak of a trade deal being strengthened by the protection of the beating heart of Sutanda. I believe this may be in reference to the Arcanum Disc, and it is what led the Mayans to help in the civil war which unseated the conquerors."

"And why are you telling me all of this?"

"I am too old to get stuck in with the physical side of archaeology now, but I do not want my previous efforts to be for nothing. I want you to take a small expedition to the island and check it out, to give an old man some closure on whether or not his hunch is correct."

Arthur slowly turned and smiled. "Sure, why not. It sounds interesting, and at the very least, I can enjoy some sun while there."

"Fantastic, and don't worry about the cost of getting there, I will cover it. Now go, get yourself ready, it's going to be an adventure I am sure!"

"Alright, I will speak to a few people and get a date together; then I will let you know who is available and when."

"That sounds great to me. Oh, and don't worry about any consequences from what happened back in Rome. I have a few contacts with the police there, and this will all be taken care of," Franklyn reassured.

"I appreciate that; thank you," Arthur said, extending his arm and shaking Franklyn's hand.

"Be seeing you," Franklyn responded with a smile.

Arthur headed out of the room and towards the exit. He was very intrigued by the conversation he had just had and still stunned at how the previous twenty-four hours had changed so much for him in such little time. He had a few calls to make and lots of preparation to do.

Alexander felt strong discomfort as the uninterrupted gaze of the man he was supposed to deliver the briefcase to bore down on him from across the table. A well-built individual who was sharply dressed, Marcus Lake had entrusted Alexander with obtaining the briefcase and ensuring it made its way to him without any issue. But this wasn't the case.

Things had not gone smoothly, and now what should have been a simple exchange had got very messy. Marcus looked down with a slight sigh and then looked up again, placing both his arms on the table and looking directly at Alexander, whose face was still bruised from what happened earlier on.

"The acquiring of the briefcase went well, without a hitch you say. You didn't get seen, no alarms were set off and you say you didn't leave any evidence other than the briefcase being taken. Am I correct so far?" Marcus slowly asked in a soft but menacing tone.

"Yes, yes sir."

"And you headed straight to Rome to meet my associates, yes?"

"That is correct."

"THEN WHAT THE BLOODY HELL HAPPENED ON YOUR WAY?" he shouted, banging the desk hard with his right hand.

The room became deathly silent for a few moments as Alexander had all the events of the previous night rush through his head.

"It was him. He was there and ruined everything. He knew who I was, and what I had. He knew it all."

"Him? There was only one person?" Marcus said in slight disbelief.

Alexander began to describe in detail what happened in Rome, from the moment he realised he was being followed at the station right up until the moment he passed out after the fight.

"Who the hell was this; did he give any indication whatsoever?"

"No. When I asked who he was he said it didn't matter, but that what I had stolen had to be returned without question. It was as if he had been sent by whoever you asked me to steal from."

"And what did he look like, any striking features? He has complicated things, and I need to find him."

"He was around 5'8", early forties, had short brown hair, brown eyes, stubble and was dressed in a short leather jacket, dark top and trousers. He spoke with an English accent, and I had never seen him before."

"You are going to help me find this man, Alexander. He has made fools of us, and this cannot go unanswered. I will arrange for my contacts to try and get us CCTV of what happened. If we have no luck, we may have to pay our friend, The Collector, a visit and see if he can shed any light on this mysterious individual and the whereabouts of that briefcase. I don't want to, as it will directly link myself to this debacle, but what is at stake is far too important."

"I swear I will not rest until this man is found, and we get our hands back on the contents of that case."

"Very well, Alexander. Now leave me, I have some calls to make. I fear this is going to get a lot bloodier before it is over."

Chapter Three

The sea breeze coolly crossed Arthur's face as he looked upon the oncoming stretch of bright, tropical land fast approaching. He was with two long-time friends, Thomas Moyes and Samuel Jones, who had the same appetite for adventure as he did. The former was someone he had served in the military with many years ago and had formed a close friendship that had lasted to this day. The latter was a man in the shipping industry who was always on hand to help transport Arthur around if the journey was to be made by sea to any of the remote locations he had been in need of reaching.

"So this is it?" Thomas asked, briefly putting his hand on Arthur's shoulder. "The place where the treasure hunt really begins?"

"Franklyn seemed certain. He says the Mayan links are strong, and this is one of the rare places where there are Mayan ruins that are not flocked with visitors."

"Well, I am all for it. This weather is beautiful," he said, smiling out to the sea, which was a calm and deep blue with the sunlight shimmering along the surface.

"I couldn't agree more."

They soon reached the shoreline, and the boat came to a halt along some low rocks, which were a metre or so above the sea level.

"The water is deep enough that I can leave the boat here without any need of you guys swimming to shore. We don't want you getting eaten by sharks now!" Samuel joked, walking over to them as they stood by the edge of the boat.

"Are you not going to come along with us?" asked Thomas.

"Best not lad, besides, if you find any Mayans angry at your trespass, I will be on standby for the getaway," he said with a smile. "On with you now."

Arthur and Thomas nodded before climbing up one at a time out of the boat and onto the land. They headed inland and could see almost instantly a large temple ruin rise above the treeline.

"That looks to be what we are here for. Let's head for that," Arthur said pointing ahead for Thomas to see.

"Then let's head for it!"

The two men walked into the treeline and the ground began to slightly ascend, indicating they were heading the right way.

"So what do you make of the story Franklyn told you; do you believe it?" Thomas asked.

"I would like to think it has some truth to it, yes. But these kinds of things are like Chinese whispers that have been passed down through hundreds of generations. So although I do not doubt that Sutanda, Mahindra and the war really happened, with regard to the amount of lost treasure and there being an undiscovered island, I am not one hundred per cent."

"But as there is still a chance, we want to be the ones to grab the fame?"

"Well, you can't say it wouldn't be nice now."

"True, I can't disagree with that!"

"I guess as I have such a high level of respect for Franklyn, all he has accomplished, and most importantly done for me, I can take him seriously. The level of passion he displayed was really something."

"Well, I am all in. Look ahead, we are almost there." Thomas observed, pointing ahead. In front of them through the break in the trees, they could see the stone steps that led up and into the temple they saw from the boat.

A minute or so later, they reached the temple, which was breath-taking. Although crumbled and weathered, it towered forty feet high and was almost pyramid-like with stone patterns and engravings covering its exterior. It cut a very impressive stature and gave the impression that even after thousands of years, this was still very much Mayan land. The steps themselves that were in front of them climbed about halfway and went into a dark void.

"Look, there is an opening about twenty feet up there. Do you want to take a look?" asked Arthur.

"Sure, sounds good to me. Even if there is nothing there, I have always wanted to check a deserted Mayan temple. Let's go," grinned Thomas.

The two men climbed the uneven steep steps and reached the opening. They walked in and saw a large oval room with various faded engravings on the rear wall. Arthur walked over and ran his fingers along one of them, trying to trace the shape of the once clear depiction.

"Amazing," he said slowly under his breath, letting go of the wall and stepping back.

"Look to your right, there seems to be a set of steps that lead down. We should check it out."

"Okay, sounds a good idea."

They moved to the edge of the room and saw an opening, which had some steps, these larger and less steep than those outside, that led down into the darkness.

"Did you bring a light?" Thomas asked.

"Yeah, I have a flashlight, yourself?"

"I do yes."

"Okay good, follow me, and be careful," said Arthur.

The two men began to slowly descend the stairs into the unknown. The walls that surrounded them were bare and gave no indication as to what was to come. As they reached the bottom, they shined the torchlight forward and could see evidence of some sort of religious chamber, with a mess of assorted minor artefacts across the floor.

At the back end of the room, a dirty but still clearly golden structure around table height supported a box, which had been struck with something heavy and broken open. Arthur walked over and looked inside and saw nothing, but a few gold coins that were too new to be of anything Mayan. He picked one up and checked it.

"These coins, they are nothing like what was from the period; they look more fourteenth or fifteenth century."

"I think something was here, in this case, and it was taken. I believe that what we are looking for was here, but we are about six hundred years too late," Thomas added, examining the area.

"Look, by either side of the golden structure, there are ripped and faded flags and banners. I can't believe I didn't notice the second we walked in," said Arthur.

He picked one up and had a closer look. It was a simple white and red insignia on black fabric.

"This flag is intended as a statement, to show who raided this room. Whoever it was wanted the world to know, it was they who got the treasure. Looks like they took everything judging by the mess in here."

"So what does this mean? Franklyn was telling the truth?" asked Thomas.

"It is possible that he found this place by finding the same clues whoever has come here before we did. I think he was onto something for sure."

"I don't think the lead is dead, not for a moment."

"How so?"

"These banners clearly show who was here. We should go and research that insignia, and what will help with that is the coins that have been left here in the box, replacing what I am to assume was an Arcanum Disc piece."

"You are right. We should find out who the insignia belongs to and see if any historical evidence shows who it may have been. Good idea, Thomas."

"Right, pick up a few of those coins. I will round up a few items with the symbol on, and we can get back to Samuel. It will be a good idea actually to arrange a meeting with Franklyn. As he has been the one looking into this over the years, maybe he has an idea of who the banners belong to."

"Good idea, let's get back. I have got to say; this has peaked my interest a lot more seeing someone else has already been on this little hunt we are now privy to," said Arthur.

With that, the two men left and headed back to the boat. On the return journey, they spoke of what they had seen with Samuel, and once they returned to the mainland, Arthur called Franklyn to tell of the news. As the phone dialled out, Arthur got a little burst of excitement, which reached a peak as the phone was picked up at the other end.

"Hello?"

"Franklyn, it's Arthur."

"Arthur, it is good to hear from you, how is the expedition going?"

"We are already done and heading home. It was a lot quicker than expected, but we have news."

"You are done already?" said Franklyn, a little stunned.

"Yeah, and we found something. It wasn't the Arcanum Disc, but I think you will be eager to see it. Are you able to meet me and Thomas back at my place in two days' time, say around noon?"

"Okay, I will be there. But is there no way you can say over the phone what you have found?"

"It will be worth the wait, I assure you."

"Alright then, get home as quick as you can, and have a safe journey."

"Thanks, we shall see you soon."

A few days passed by, and Thomas and Arthur were sat in the front room of Arthur's home, awaiting the knock at the door.

The home, which was nestled in the outskirts of a quintessential English village in the South, was full of quirky trinkets and treasures that had been clearly collected from his travels around the world.

After a few minutes of general conversation, a car could be heard pulling up outside, which was soon followed by a loud knock. Arthur made his way to the door and opened it and greeted Franklyn.

"Franklyn, thank you for coming."

"It is my pleasure. I must say after your tease of information the other day this visit couldn't have come soon enough."

"Can I get you anything before we get down to business? A drink perhaps?"

"I am okay, thank you. Where to?"

"I have everything set up in the study, please follow me."

Arthur ushered him through the hall where Thomas joined them, and they began walking up the stairs towards his study. Here, they had laid out the banners and coins on a large table ready for presentation.

"So, what did you find on that island, just Mayan ruins or something more as I suspect?" asked Franklyn.

"Well, as discussed previously, it wasn't the Arcanum Disc we found; however, we did find a vault that was hidden deep within a Mayan temple ruin. Inside were assorted items from the period, nothing noteworthy. However, at the back of the room was a large golden table that had a smashed ruin of a chest on top."

"We believe this was where the Arcanum Disc piece once was. There was a set of faded illustrations above the chest that showed a small almost ancient comic strip of three images, showing allies handing over an item that was placed under Mayan protection," added Thomas.

Mid conversation, they entered the study, and everything found was on display.

"As you can see, we have laid out all that we found for you to have a look," advised Arthur, extending his hand towards the table.

Franklyn walked forward and began to examine the items, running his fingers over the banner and looking deep in thought.

"At first, we thought that as the Arcanum Disc piece wasn't present that the trail ended there, but then we got thinking about these banners, and how they appear to have been left by whoever took the treasure as a sort of calling card," Thomas explained.

"Exactly, and as they had left it, the next logical step is to find out what the banners reflect and trace them, to see if any treasure finds were publicised," Arthur added.

"We appreciate it is a long shot, but we think that is the best thing to do. What do you make of them, do you have any ideas?"

Franklyn looked over the items a little more and then spoke softly.

"It does look very familiar to me. Let me think. Yes, I have got it!"

"You do?" Arthur said, surprised.

"Yes. Have you ever heard of Captain James Turner?"

"I can't say I have, how about you Thomas?" asked Arthur.

"No. Please enlighten us."

"Captain James Turner was a pirate at around the same time as Thomas Avery in what is referred to as The Golden Age, and his infamous career really began in around 1794 when he was drafted as a privateer by King William III of England. He successfully took out enemy fleets on the order of the monarchy and returned great riches for them, of which he received a small percentage. However, as his experience and skills grew, he grew tired of the small percentages he received as rewards and began to disobey. He would hide large portions of loot and keep it from the state; however, these actions made him become outlawed and a wanted man."

"Sounds quite the typical pirate so far," Thomas remarked.

"Yes, true. However, this is where the tale gets interesting. Fleeing with his crew, they all decided to go after much bigger prizes and to remain undetected they stopped attacking other ships and instead aimed at discovering treasure for themselves. The coins here alongside the banners are his, so it would suggest that they had found one of the Arcanum Disc pieces and were possibly looking for more. But where did they go after this, and where on earth did the treasure they looted end up? This is going to need some looking into, some detailed research into this individual and his exploits."

"So we need to see if anything was reported, written about or indeed written by the pirates themselves about big treasure loots?" asked Arthur thoughtfully.

"Precisely. I will have a look through my archive, but I would recommend you have a dig around yourselves. May I take one of these banners with me?" enquired Franklyn.

"Of course, please do," Arthur encouraged.

With this, Franklyn said his goodbyes, and he gave Thomas a lift back towards the city. Arthur closed the door and immediately began thinking of where to start his research.

He spent the next three or so days in and out of archives, libraries and museums, piecing together the tales of the fabled James Turner and searching for anything even with a passing reference to a treasure find in the Caribbean.

A stroke of luck came when Arthur found a copy of a letter that was written by the pirate that revealed it all. You had to read it with the knowledge Arthur had to understand, but it was there, plain to see. He picked up his phone and called Thomas.

"It took a while connecting the dots between the various stories and documents in the public domain, but I have found something out that I think you will want to hear."

"About Turner? Okay, shoot."

"Turner and his crew began a search for the Arcanum Disc pieces after hearing whispers and tales about them from various pirates they had come across on their adventures. They were seemingly well aware of what they were looking for when they raided that Mayan tomb, and on the return journey from that tomb to their hideout, the pirates were attacked by a small section of the King's navy. Turner won the battle, but the ship carrying the Arcanum Disc was sunk. He returned with just the one ship left and was furious.

"The King got word of the defeat but, as it confirmed the Captain's whereabouts, sent a larger fleet to the location, and Turner was captured and brought to England for trial. He was locked up, and while imprisoned, Turner wrote the letters outlining the story of what had happened and how he had lost the Arcanum Disc piece through the battle he fought against the royal navy. He was soon executed, but his legacy was set, and the tales of his adventures became synonymous with the word Pirate."

"So, if we want to carry on this crazy search, we now need to go searching for a missing shipwreck?" Thomas asked excitedly.

"Yep, seems that way."

"Jones is going to love us, needing his boat again so soon. But where are we going to look?"

"I think I have that covered as well. Turner's hideout is now widely known to have been on the British Virgin Islands. Multiple evidence of a small settled colony of pirates have been discovered there and logs from King William III's navy showed numerous battles on record as being around 20 miles southwest of the Virgin Islands in the Caribbean Sea."

"So as Franklyn told it, that is where Turner was ambushed by the British Navy?"

"That is right. As we know, he was defeated but wrote of losing a ship that contained a valuable treasure. As it was the return journey from the Mayan ruin near Yucatán, I am willing to bet good money that this is where we will find the Arcanum Disc piece."

"Right okay, I am all for it. When do you want to go diving?" Thomas asked.

"Ideally as soon as possible. Let's speak to Samuel and get some equipment sorted. Once that is done, I can't see any reason to delay."

Chapter Four

Arthur looked up towards the clear blue sky, admiring the peacefulness of the cloudless air above. He looked down after a few moments and then to his right. Thomas was sat, as he was, on the edge of the boat with his legs over, moving them slowly up and down. They were in full diving gear and ready to go under.

Thomas looked at Arthur and gave him a thumb up, which Arthur reciprocated. With this, Thomas dropped over board and into the water. Arthur looked down at the sea, which was as clear as the sky and then thrust his body off the boat. A moment of airtime was achieved before splashing into the water below. They had checked records, and a wreck of an ancient ship had been found below them at this location but had never been physically explored by anyone due to being discovered via sonar by chance.

Scientists had been scanning the seabed for the understanding of the differences in material and texture type that were below and had picked it up on their scans. Arthur looked back up at the boat, and Samuel came into view throwing a large rope into the water for the men to use to safely dive and re-ascend in the same place. Arthur nodded and then looked over to Thomas.

"Ready to go?" he asked, via the communication radio the two men had between the two diving helmets.

"You bet," Thomas replied before beginning his dive.

Arthur followed and began slowly moving himself deeper down via the rope.

"If this even is the ship, what are we expecting the condition to be? Surely anything that has been down here that long would have fallen apart?" asked Thomas.

"I have no idea. It really depends. I mean, it has been down here for what, over two hundred years, so anything could have happened."

"Yeah, you are right."

"However, remember the Mary Rosc? That was under water for four hundred and thirty-seven years when it was raised, and it still resembled a ship, so there is hope."

They soon reached a depth that was getting quite dim, so they put on the strong torchlights they had on the top of their helmets. A little further down, where it was becoming harder to pull their bodies down via the rope, the seabed came into view.

"I can't see anything; what way do you think we should go?" asked Arthur.

"Hmm, the sonar images were here, give or take twenty metres or so in either direction. We should count paces in either direction, starting opposite from each other, and see what we find."

Arthur looked down at his arm and checked the direction on the compass.

"Okay, I will go behind me, which is north. If you head south, we can both count approximately the distance we need, and then if we find nothing, come back here."

"Sure," agreed Thomas before turning and walking off. Arthur did the same, and as he got around halfway, he turned his head to look back and could see absolutely nothing. He was surprised at how short the field of vision was without direct light. Arthur found nothing so began to turn back.

"Negative my end."

"Same here, heading back to you now."

The two men met and then did the same but with east and west directions. Looking down at the never-changing seabed of sand and the occasional weed sticking through, Arthur began to lose himself in thought. He started to wonder if all of this was actually going to be worth the time invested, or if it was just chasing an old fantasy.

That moment of doubt, however, didn't last long, as some wooden beams came into view. Arthur looked up and stopped in his tracks. Pure childlike wonder hit him, and as chills shot down his spine and through his body, he pressed the button on the side of his helmet to speak to Thomas.

"Thomas. I have found something you will want to see. Head back in the opposite direction from you and come find me."

"I am heading over now. What is it?" he asked.

"I am going to let you be the judge of that."

Around thirty seconds later, Thomas arrived and Arthur looked back to greet him, and then they both aimed their gaze forward.

"Incredible!" Thomas said, with his eyes wide open, taking it in. Ahead of them was a shipwreck, not large by any means but impressive nonetheless. They were at the front of the wreck, and it was firmly wedged at a thirty to forty-degree angle in the seabed.

The front had its right side, which would have been out of the ground missing, and as a result, the hull was wide open. This was a likely combination of the damage sustained from the battle hundreds of years ago but also from the impact of smashing into the seabed.

"Do you think this is it?" asked Thomas.

"Without a doubt, this is what was picked up on the sonar. Let's go and take a look inside."

The two men slowly moved to the large opening at the front and stepped inside. They knew they could not venture too far inside with the rope as it would get tangled. Reaching the last part of the ship that was broken open, they moved carefully as to not get the rope, which was their lifeline to Samuel's ship, tangled on anything, the broken wooden beams being an immediate concern.

"Here, hold my rope a second; I think I see something just inside that remains of what appears to be a cabin," Arthur said to Thomas, who agreed and took the rope from Arthur. He watched as Arthur disappeared into a void in the ship interior. A few moments of silence passed before he stuck his head out with a smile.

"You remember in the letter that a reference to a golden soul was made?"

"Vaguely yes, why?"

"Well, there is a golden chest in here with a faded but still legible set of initials on. I will let you guess what they are."

"J.T.?"

"Ding ding! We have a winner!"

"No way! We can't open it down here though, right?"

"Unfortunately not, we need to get it to the surface to take a look. It has a lock on it that, although weak, we can't break without some sort of blunt object. I can get it out of here, but I will need help to carry it. I think if we get it back to the spot above the ship, we can get Samuel to bring a crane down and carry it to the surface."

"Okay, agreed."

Arthur then began to carry, although clearly with a struggle, the chest out towards Thomas. He reached him, and both men took an end of it and lightened the load. They then carried it slowly back from where they came, and once the rope became completely vertical with no bend, they knew they were in the right place.

"Samuel, do you read me?" Arthur radioed up.

"Loud and clear. Finished playing down there?" Samuel joked.

"Yeah, and we have a new toy box we want to open. Can you send down your crane, so we can get it up to have a look?"

"Sure, give me a moment, and I will release it."

Around half a minute later, slowly through the darkness came a small crane with a platform attached.

"Are you clear?" Samuel asked as the crane came within ten metres or so from the bottom.

"Yeah, all clear. Bring her down," confirmed Thomas.

With that, the platform hit the bottom, and both men climbed on it and placed the chest down. There was enough room for them both to ascend with it, so they remained in place.

"Okay, ready to come back. Bring us up."

"Roger that."

The crane shuddered slightly and then began to climb back to the surface. As the light began to fill the water around them, both men turned off the torches on their helmets. Arthur looked up, and as he did, the water changed into the sun and fresh air of the water level. He waved to Samuel, who hoisted them back onto the deck. They walked a few steps forward, taking their helmets off and breathing in the fresh sea air.

"Do you have a crowbar or anything on board? This thing looks like it could do with a little bit of a forceful introduction," asked Arthur.

"Here, I heard you guys on the radio down there, so I had it on standby," Samuel said, holding a large crowbar out. "Who wants the honours?"

"You go for it, Thomas, bust it open," said Arthur.

"Okay, thanks!" replied Thomas with a smile.

He knelt down on one knee and began by knocking it a few times. There was no movement, so he placed the jagged end of the crowbar around the lock and pulled down hard on one end of it. It soon broke open, and water came pouring out as the pressure was released that had built up over all the years of submersion. With anticipation building, Thomas lifted the lid and pushed it back, revealing what James Turner had found that fabled day. It was truly a sight to behold, and one that everyone instantly realised the magnitude of what the pirates fought for.

"Is that…" Thomas stuttered, picking up the artefact and bringing it into the sunlight.

"I think it is. It matches the descriptions of what we have read up to this point, and it looks to have two parts missing," replied Arthur.

Smiles spread amongst the men as they felt the first real accomplishment. This was the moment that they realised there was more to what Franklyn had told them than just myth. It was now that they truly believed that the story could be real, and they couldn't help but have the tale of Arcanum take hold.

"I'm going to give Franklyn a call, to tell him the good news," Arthur said, walking inside the ship to grab his phone.

Chapter Five

A loud set of three knocks rang out from the front door and caught Franklyn off guard. He wasn't expecting anyone, not at this hour. It was late, close to midnight, and he was just finishing up his usual reading until the knock. He tried to ignore it at first, but another set of knocks, louder still, rang out within a few seconds of the last.

Franklyn stood up and went downstairs towards the door. He walked up to the door and looked through the spy hole. Two men were on his doorstep, and he recognised one, Marcus Lake. He felt a little confusion, but this replaced the brief concern he had previously felt. He knew Marcus from his years of artefact research in Rome. He opened the door and stood in front of them.

"Marcus?" asked Franklyn.

"Yes. Hello, Franklyn. I am sorry to call at such an unsociable hour, but I need to speak with you."

"Of course."

"May I come in? This won't take long, I assure you."

"Okay, please."

The two men walked in, and Marcus closed the door behind him.

"I was in Rome recently, a few days ago actually, and I was waiting for a delivery. Something that I had with a very trusted courier who I had every faith would deliver on time."

"Okay…" Franklyn said, confused.

"The courier was this man beside me you see today. He was intercepted by a man who attacked him and said that the item had to be returned from where it came."

"I am sorry, Marcus, but you have lost me."

"Okay, let me come straight out with it. This item was a briefcase. It had something inside it that would help locate a rare artefact, one that I know that you are heavily invested in. Does this ring any bells Franklyn?"

"Regarding the Arcanum Disc?"

"Still quite the bright spark I see, yes that is the one. Normally, I usually wouldn't own up to something like this, but time is really tight on this one. I arranged for this gentleman on my right to come here a few nights ago and take that briefcase and bring it to me. You had previously refused me copies of the documents, and I had no real choice. However, as previously mentioned, he was attacked by someone sent by you, and I have come to take back what was due to me. Where is it?"

"You bastard. You absolute vile bastard!" snapped Franklyn, realising what had happened.

"Now Franklyn, there is no need for that. I will only ask once more, where is it?"

"Go to hell and get out of my house immediately!"

"Fine, I wanted to be civil about all this. Alexander, go look where you first acquired this briefcase."

Alexander nodded and immediately went upstairs and towards the study. Franklyn followed straight away, and Marcus a moment later.

"Stop! You have no right being here, if you don't leave right this instant I will call the police!"

They entered the study, and Franklyn turned to Marcus as Alexander went into another room.

"There isn't any such briefcase here, I assure you."

"Don't lie. The man who intercepted it made it quite clear it was to be returned here. Now, where is it?"

"I am telling the truth!"

Alexander came back into the room and looked towards Marcus.

"Well?"

"It isn't here. The room is as I left it, no change."

"How very disappointing."

"I told you!"

"Shut up. This just leads to my second line of enquiry. Who did you send to retrieve the briefcase? Who was the man who caused this very visit here tonight?"

"I will never tell you. Yes, I did order its retrieval, but it is not here. Do you think I would be so stupid?"

"Fine, then he has it."

"He does, and you will never get your hands on it. I have entrusted the search to someone other than myself."

"You will tell me who this man is, or there will be very grave consequences. Do not push me, Franklyn. I will ask once more, who is the man with whom the briefcase is, and where can I find it?"

"Go to hell!"

Marcus' patience ran out, and he struck Franklyn once across the face, knocking him back into his desk.

"TELL ME! WHERE IS THE BRIEFCASE?" shouted Marcus.

"I will never tell you! I spent a great deal of my life looking for it, and I will not give it up to a common thief like you!"

"Alexander, search this room, starting with his desk. There must be some kind of evidence of who this man is."

Alexander began searching the desk, and the few documents and letters that littered its top.

"There is a diary here open with a few notes regarding a trip to Rome for 'AK' but that is all."

"AK. AK Franklyn. Whose initials are these?"

"None of your business, Marcus; you will never find out."

"Oh really?" he replied before hitting him again, knocking him down to the floor. "You are going to tell me, Franklyn. I will not leave this property until you do."

"Then I hope you brought a sleeping bag."

"You sarcastic old fool. Do you think this is a game?" said Marcus before picking him up and pushing against the wall beside the desk. "Well, do you?"

The room fell silent for a moment until it was interrupted by the telephone ringing from Franklyn's desk. It rang for a little while before going to voicemail. A voice sounded out through the small speaker on the phone unit, and as it started to speak, Franklyn felt incredibly deflated. It was Arthur.

"Franklyn? It's Arthur. I have some news, make sure you are sat down. Right, ready? We found it; we actually found it. We discovered an old shipwreck in the Caribbean Sea southwest of the Virgin Islands and dived down and sure enough, in one of the chests was a piece of the Arcanum Disc. Would you believe that? We are going to look straight into where the next piece is, and I will call you again. Speak to you soon." The phone line beeped and then cut off.

"Arthur. That is him, isn't it? Arthur. You gave him the information from the briefcase, and he has ALREADY FOUND A PIECE OF IT?" he shouted, striking him once more. He threw him to the ground and walked a few paces away, furious.

"It is in rightful hands now. Arthur is a better archaeologist than me and more skilled than you would ever know. If anyone is to find the complete artefact and the treasure it is hiding, then he is the man who deserves it."

"Deserves it? I have spent years trying to find it and even asked you for the documents politely, but you declined. Oh, what a mistake you made when you decided that. That is enough to infuriate me, but the fact you had them taken back from me and then have given all the information to this Arthur who has already found a piece? You have one final chance, tell me where to find him or I swear it will be the last mistake you ever make."

Franklyn spat on the floor by Marcus' feet and looked him in the eyes defiantly.

"I will never tell you. You don't deserve to find that treasure; you are not worthy of it."

Marcus looked him coldly in the face before picking him up by the throat and pushing him against the wall. He drew a knife from his jacket and stabbed Franklyn deep into his side. Franklyn's eyes widened, and he looked in disbelief at Marcus.

"Fine, we will do this the hard way," Marcus said, twisting the knife and withdrawing it. Franklyn fell to the floor and collapsed in an ever-growing pool of his own blood.

"Alexander, we need to take note of the number that called the phone, and need to gain access to the voicemail so if he rings again, we can keep track of his progress. He is bound to leave another, as our dear friend Franklyn will be in no position to ever speak to him again."

"No problem," Alexander said, taking the details down from the answering machine.

Marcus knelt down and looked Franklyn in the eyes.

"You had to die, you know that. If you had lived, you would have told Arthur about our little visit today and warned him we were coming for him. But now we know a bit more about him, and he doesn't know who we are. I will find him, and I will take back what is mine, and just like you, he won't be able to stop me.

"I guess I should be grateful to you for putting this chain of events in motion. Arthur has done some of the heavy lifting for me, and I will be sure to thank him for that. Goodbye, Franklyn."

Marcus stood back up and left the room with Alexander behind him. Franklyn, in his blurring vision, saw the two men vanish down the stairs and as the thud of the front door closing reverberated around the room, his vision failed, and he died.

Chapter Six

Arthur looked up from the seemingly endless paperwork strewn across his desk and saw two familiar faces looking back at him in photos. One was of his late wife Pamela. The photo was one taken a short while before they were married and captured a playful smile with a sunny and tropical backdrop. It was one of his favourites and reminded him of the good times they had together, a snapshot he could always dive back into and relive the moment.

The other photo was of his young daughter Olivia, a recent snap at her latest birthday party where she had a huge grin across her face. He smiled to himself and turned the page. He was looking over more copies of the various journals James Turner had written, trawling for clues. A few moments passed, and a flurry of footsteps came towards his desk.

Onto the page, he was reading a folded piece of brown paper was placed followed by a little giggle. He looked up and saw Olivia standing before him, deep blue eyes lit up with excitement with her long brown hair down in a messy fashion. She was eleven years old and full of spirit and really reminded him of a younger Pamela.

"What is this?" Arthur asked Olivia.

"I did some investigating after the story last night, and I have found it!"

"Found what?"

"Something to help you find what you are looking for, open it!" Olivia said excitedly, gesturing towards the paper.

He opened the paper, and it unfolded to be a hand-drawn treasure map, with a big X in what appeared to be an outline of the garden.

"A map?"

"Yep! I found a map which shows where a really important clue is, come on, we need to go and get it!"

"Okay, let's go on a little adventure!" Arthur said, getting up from his desk.

Olivia ran off straight away and Arthur tried to keep up. He walked through the hall and to the top of the stairs and saw her waiting for him at the bottom. She looked up and smiled before running off again.

"Too slow!" she shouted, as she ran through the kitchen and into the back garden.

Arthur went out into the garden and appreciated the cool fresh breeze that hit him. He had been in the study for a few hours, and the break was welcome. He saw Olivia a short distance away, jumping up and down. He looked down at the map and saw a big red X drawn by a tree, so he headed towards the largest tree in the corner of the garden where Olivia's tree house was.

"Have you worked out where it is yet?" Olivia asked.

Arthur looked down and saw a freshly disturbed level of soil, with a spade nearby.

"I think this is a good place to look; what do you think?"

"Yes, you need this!" Olivia said, handing him the spade.

"Thanks," Arthur replied, as he got down and started digging. A few moments later, a little box appeared in the shallow hole. It was around a metre by half a metre and burgundy in colour.

"That's it, that's it!" Olivia excitedly proclaimed.

"Let's take a look," Arthur said, placing the box on the ground and sitting on the grass. He opened it, and inside was another folded piece of paper. He unfolded this, and saw it was a drawing Olivia had created. It showed a ship on an ocean with two figures on it, a huge sun in the sky with a smiley face and an island with an opened treasure chest on the right.

"Wow, this is incredible! Do you know what it is?" Arthur asked.

Olivia came over and sat next to him, pointing at the drawing.

"It is you and I on a big boat on a treasure hunt looking for the island you told me about last night. The sun in the sky is Mum, and she is showing us where to go!"

Arthur felt a nice warm wave of emotion rush through him as he took a second look at the drawing knowing what it was of. He never knew after reading a story about Atlantis last night and then saying he was looking for somewhere just like it would capture her imagination so much.

"This is really helpful; it will definitely help show where to go, thank you."

"That's okay."

"Now, do you fancy some lunch? All this treasure hunting has made me very hungry!"

"Yes, please. The last one to the kitchen is a rotten egg!" Olivia shouted, already running off into the distance.

Arthur smiled and began walking after her, placing the drawing neatly alongside the map in his back pocket. He was definitely happy to be home.

A few more days passed by with a balance of keeping Olivia happy and looking over the journals for any clue. At the suggestion of Thomas, he had gone back through the letters of James Turner and discovered a key passage of text that spoke of an Arcanum Disc piece being hidden in the snowy mountains of North-East Greenland. He was certain this was a lead worthy of investigation, so-called Thomas.

Unfortunately, Thomas was off helping Samuel so they were not free for a few weeks, but Arthur had the urge to go explore the area, so decided to head up alone with the promise of updating Thomas as he went on. Thomas was happy with it, being kept in the loop while avoiding the cold.

Since Pamela had passed away a few years ago, whenever Arthur was away she was cared for by Martha West. She was a family friend and godparent to Olivia and had become a key figure in her life. Arthur arranged for her to return the following morning. It was bothering him how he hadn't heard back from Franklyn, so he called once more. Disappointed it again went straight to voicemail, he left him another message.

"Hey, Franklyn. Haven't heard from you in a little while so getting a little worried, give me a call as soon as you get this message ok? Just a quick one to say I am heading to Greenland to investigate a lead I found in the letters of James Turner. Seems he had a suspicion that there was a piece in the mountains of North-East Greenland but didn't have the resource to get there at the time. I am going to check it out and will keep you posted. Call me when you can."

Arthur put the phone down and tried to put the worry to the back of his mind, as he had a long journey ahead the next day.

The tape emitted a beep and then stopped, indicating the end of the voicemail. Marcus looked up at Alexander with a smile. It was the recording that changed everything. They knew where Arthur was heading next, and they intended on finding him.

Chapter Seven

"Mr King, it is good to see you. Pleasant journey I hope?"

"It was indeed; thank you, Tikaani."

Arthur was meeting an Inuit male known as Atka Tikaani, which meant King Wolf. He had obtained the right to this title within the people here as he was one of the best hunters for food within the community. He was singled out to Arthur as the perfect person to guide him through the icy cold terrain and to the caverns he wanted to explore.

"I have got us a snowmobile each so we can navigate the terrain better. It will get us to the caverns with no problem. I have also taken the liberty of getting a pair of climbing axes so we can climb the more tricky parts that are common with the caverns we have marked as sites of interest."

"Fantastic, thank you. I have got some food supplies for us to consume while we are out as well."

"What's that on your back?" asked Arthur.

"It's a rifle, just in case we encounter any bears."

"Wise, but as long as we stay away, we should not have any problems. You shouldn't need it."

"I hope you are right. Come with me, what we will do is drop off your things at the cabin, go through the plan for the exploration and then get ready."

With that, Arthur was helped by another individual and shown to the cabin which was a few-minute walk into the settlement. In there, he placed his things away and was shown his room before being directed to the main room with a table in the centre. Here, Tikaani had already placed a map with a few red circles on it to the north of their location.

"As you can see here by my red markings, the caverns that you have outlined are here. They are quite far north, and as a result, they have never been visited as far as I am aware, not by anyone from our community anyway."

"Great, adds a level of excitement if we reach it for sure."

"Indeed. Now, the weather is calm today, so it is preferable we leave within the next few hours if you are happy with that of course."

"Yes, I am, ready to go whenever you are."

"Okay, good. I shall go and prepare the snowmobiles and ensure everything is set. I will come back for you in an hour or so."

With that, Tikaani left and Arthur went through his main bag and placed what he needed into the smaller expedition bag. He wished Thomas could be there for the adventure, but he was happy to have the company of Tikaani, as having someone beside him who knew the environment as well as he did was essential.

Just over an hour later, there was a knock at the door. Arthur looked out of the cabin window next to the door and saw Tikaani smiling with his thumb up, indicating it was time to leave. Arthur nodded, grabbed his bag and went outside to meet him. They walked a short distance across from the cabin and came to the snowmobiles; both set up and ready to go.

"The one on the left is for you. I assume you have experience in using one of these?"

"Yes, I used to go for rides in Greenland so I'm quite familiar."

"Excellent. The terrain should be very similar to what you are used to. We are heading north along the coast first before heading further inland a few miles up."

"Okay, sounds good to me."

"I will lead. Are you ready to go?" asked Tikaani.

Arthur turned the engine on and looked up with a smile.

"Yeah, ready to go!"

"Okay, let's go have an adventure."

Tikaani revved up his engine and then moved off, with Arthur close behind. They slowly drove through the settlement of colourful little wooden huts and then hit a flat section of snow, which was essentially a makeshift road where it has been driven on so many times by snowmobiles. It was here they picked up speed and soon they were travelling on smooth snow alongside the icy waters on their right. Arthur couldn't help but marvel at the beautiful environment he was in.

On his right was the calm water of the ocean dotted by lumps of ice and ahead were snowy mountains as far as the eye could see, with the sun just behind the highest peak, shining across the blanket of perfectly dusted snow. It was moments like this he regretted not having a camera to hand. After half an hour, they passed through a small but dense set of trees, standing tall and coated with snow before reaching the base of a large mountain. Tikaani gestured to Arthur to stop, and they did so. Arthur looked up and could see a set of mountains close to each other. He had a feeling that this was it for the snowmobiles, and the rest of the journey would be on foot.

"The cavern that you want to explore, it is up there," Tikaani said, pointing upwards. "We can make it easily by foot as it isn't too steep. Are you ready?"

"Always, let's do it."

The two men began to ascend the mountain and were soon heading towards the area of the cavern. Arthur looked forward and could see the slight incline ahead covered in snow, which was surrounded on both sides by a rocky mountain face, which slowly increased to a great height. Arthur was grateful as it acted as a barrier to the cold wind that was getting harsher the higher they went.

"From the maps we looked over; this cavern should be around twenty to twenty-five metres ahead."

"The closer it is the better!"

"The entrance we are going for is one of two, but the other is further up on the opposite side of the mountain, so we will go for this one."

The two men walked the distance and came across a small opening in the mountain face, which was about the size of an average man standing with his arms outstretched.

"This must be it," remarked Tikaani.

"Okay, let's do this," Arthur said as Tikaani entered first. Arthur was close behind, and they took in what was ahead.

The first part of the cave was just a bare rocky space, but it led slightly downwards towards another section. They walked down and saw two very faded and worn statues, one on each side of a large break in the cavern wall.

"This is looking promising. These are definitely manmade structures that look thousands of years old."

"What are they?" Tikaani asked.

"I'm not sure. They look almost Mayan in style, with the larger heads offset by the smaller body. They each have the farthest hand down and outstretched as if offering something. I wonder what is beyond here."

"Let's keep moving. I am deeply intrigued as to what could be hidden away here."

The two men moved through the statues and into a second room, which was a passageway. On the right was a large sheet of ice that came down from the top surface around four metres up and was quite low towards the end of the passage, with around a metre and a half of space. Reaching this point, they both crouched through and stumbled into what was apparently the main chamber. In front of them was a row of three smaller statues on each side, all kneeling forward in front of a stone display at the end of a small aisle.

Arthur was lured over and walked past and in front of Tikanni up to the display. There was an empty recess, which looked to have held something that was of apparent worship. He looked forward and slightly above the display and could see faded illustrations, which appeared to show one tribe handing a glowing treasure to another for protection. Arthur wondered if this was supposed to show a small group of individuals from Sutanda presenting an Arcanum Disc piece for protection. Above the recess was what appeared to be a brief line of text in Quechuan, an ancient language spoken by ancient South American civilisations. Arthur could just make it out.

"A piece of the soul never leaves its true home. A piece of soul never leaves its true home," Arthur quietly repeated to himself a few times, thinking it over, again and again, trying to make sense of it. He turned to speak to Tikaani, but he wasn't behind him.

"Tikaani?" he asked, looking around.

"You are too late, Arthur," a deep voice echoed through the cavern.

Arthur turned to see a man he had never seen before walk out from behind a rock face near the entrance, holding an artefact in his hand. Arthur immediately recognised it as it was similar to the Arcanum Disc piece he had found from the shipwreck.

"Who are you?"

"My name is Marcus. I am the man who you stole from back in Rome. Did you really think you would get away from that with no level of response?"

"I don't know what you are talking about."

"Oh, really? Let me refresh your memory. Alexander?"

Out of the shadows came Alexander, with his gun aimed at Tikaani. Behind him were three other men, all armed, looking towards Arthur.

"Do you remember this gentleman? He remembers who you are. You chased him through Rome and took that briefcase. That briefcase was of valuable importance to me and you took it."

"You had no right. It wasn't yours."

"No? What, so it was the belonging of that old fool Franklyn?"

"How do you know him?"

"It doesn't matter. What matters is that when I paid him a little visit recently, he had no choice but to tell me all about you and how he passed his little treasure hunt on."

"What did you do?"

"He didn't spill easily. Well, not until the end anyway."

"Bastard, what have you done?"

"Let's just say he was so blindly protecting you and this Arcanum Disc artefact that he used up all of his remaining existence."

Arthur felt a mix of rage and despair run through his veins as he looked up at Marcus.

"Now, I must thank you for doing all the extra legwork for me. Finding the first piece and leading me here to this one. But it would appear that you still have something that belongs to me. Tell me, where is the first piece that you found on that shipwreck?"

"How do you know all of this?"

"You left a few very valuable voicemails, and I was happy to lend an ear to them. Now, you are going to tell me where the Arcanum Disc piece is, or I will ask Alexander here to kill your friend, and then we will make you suffer until you give me what I want. Where is it?"

"I'm not giving you anything. If you have killed Franklyn, I swear you will live to regret it."

"Oh really? You do not seem in a position to be threatening anyone right now."

Marcus was by Alexander now and walking closer to Arthur. As he got within a few feet, Arthur looked up and noticed a small fuel container with the few supplies that Marcus and his men had. He knew he had to get out of here with Tikaani, and time was running out. As Marcus got within reaching distance, Arthur grabbed his handgun and shot the fuel container which caused a small explosion.

As everyone looked around, he punched Marcus and grabbed the Arcanum Disc artefact from his grasp. As Marcus was knocked back, Tikaani backhanded Alexander in the face and took his handgun. As the explosion started a small fire, briefly distracting the armed men, Arthur and Tikaani took advantage and ran for the exit.

"AFTER THEM!" Marcus shouted.

The two men crouched under the ice sheet and then ran as fast as they could along the passage. A few rounds of machine-gun fire hit the ice wall and broke some of it away as the men on the other side aimlessly fired towards them. As Arthur and Tikaani reached the end of the passage, Arthur looked back and saw the men were crouching through and in close pursuit. Arthur ran out of the cavern, past the stone statues and out into the snow. It was snowing a little, and he hoped this would give a little cover.

As they reached the top of the mountain climb, the four men giving chase came out of the cave firing at them. This forced Arthur and Tikaani to take cover behind some of the rocks and return fire. As the men briefly stopped shooting to reload, Arthur saw the opportunity to get away and gestured to Tikaani. As they ran down the mountain and back towards the snowmobiles, Marcus came out from behind the men.

"They are getting away, after them!"

"I take it that you weren't expecting this!" Tikaani shouted to Arthur as they ran.

"Definitely not. I have never seen that guy before, and I don't want to again!"

The two men reached the snowmobiles and quickly took off, full speed away from the mountain and back in the direction they originally came from. After a minute or so, they seemed to have lost the pursuers, but then three snowmobiles came from around the other side of the mountain straight for them. One had Alexander on, one had Marcus and the other had two men. Bullets started to dance around them as the attackers fired towards Arthur and Tikaani.

Arthur turned and saw Tikaani was essentially blind firing his weapon in the hope to slow the men down. Arthur slowed slightly and then decided as he couldn't get a shot to be risky. He turned and began to drive towards them briefly and managed to get a few shots in, hitting the two men on the one snowmobile and taking them out. As he did and got a little too close to the others he turned again and sped up, gradually getting back the distance he had before, although at the cost of having to brace a hail of bullets that were a lot closer than before, with a few ricocheting off the back of the snowmobile.

Tikaani then broke away from Arthur and fired at Alexander and managed to hit his vehicle enough that it stopped in its tracks. This left just Marcus, and as they entered the wooded area, they gained a huge advantage. Not wanting to lead Marcus back to the settlement, Arthur knew he had to be stopped. He decided to play a very dangerous move and stopped the snowmobile by a few of the trees. He hopped off and took the rifle from his back and crouched, aiming it back towards where Marcus was coming.

In a few seconds, he appeared in his scope, and as a hail of bullets from Marcus wildly hit trees around him, he fired a single shot at the front of the snowmobile which took out the engine. He saw Marcus come to a halt and could see him shout in anger. With this, Arthur smiled towards Tikaani, and they both took off, speeding back towards the settlement.

A few hours had passed since they returned to the settlement, and none of the men had arrived. Tikaani had arranged for the two snowmobiles to be hidden, and he and Arthur stayed out of sight in the cabin.

"They haven't come here. Do you think we will be safe here for now?" Arthur asked.

"Yes, but we need to get you out of here and back home as soon as possible. I will make arrangements for you," said Tikaani.

"How did we not know they were heading towards the cavern? I would assume they would have come through here?"

"Not necessarily. There were a few entrances to that cavern, so it is likely they came from the north. With regard to equipment, they must have had it come from somewhere else."

"I am really sorry for everything that happened back there. I thought we would just get to explore the caverns without any issue."

"It is okay Arthur; no problem at all. Besides, it gave me quite the adrenaline rush, much better than sitting around doing nothing!"

Arthur nodded in agreement, and as he did, he felt his phone vibrate. He took it out, and it was a text message from Thomas saying to call him as soon as possible as something had happened back home. He thought back to what Marcus had said about Franklyn and began to expect it would be about that.

"I need to step out and make a call if that is okay."

"Of course, just stay behind the cabin, and you should be obscured from view."

"Okay, thank you."

Arthur stepped outside and dialled Thomas' number. It rang longer than usual and then he picked up.

"I got your message; what's up?"

"It's Franklyn. I'm really sorry."

"What's happened?"

"A few days ago, Franklyn was found at his home. He has been murdered."

"Does anyone know what happened?"

"It doesn't look like there was a forced entry or break-in, but he was found with a single deep stab wound to the side. I can't believe it."

"Neither can I, Thomas. I am returning home now, just making final arrangements, and I will be back."

"I have been notified the funeral is next week, so we should be there to show our respects."

"Yes, of course."

"How did you get on over there?"

"I will tell you about it when I am back, and we can talk face to face. I need to let what has happened to Franklyn sink in a little. I will speak to you soon."

"Okay, speak to you soon. Safe journey."

Chapter Eight

After the service for Franklyn, Arthur and Thomas stood above the coffin as it lay in the ground, ready to be buried. Thomas put his arm on Arthur's shoulder, and then the two men walked further into the graveyard.

"That was a beautiful service; he would have been happy with that," Thomas said supportively.

"Yeah, you are right."

"I hope they find out what happened to him and catch whoever did it."

"I have a feeling I already know."

"What do you mean?"

"I need to tell you about the time I had in Greenland. When I arrived, I went with the Inuit guide Tikaani into the mountains, and we checked the cavern which we suspected had the Arcanum Disc, or at the very least a connection to the Sutandan Empire. While in there, a man named Marcus, and a few armed men were there waiting for me."

"Waiting for you?"

"Yeah, it turns out that the man I intercepted in Rome, whom I now know as Alexander as he was also there in Greenland, was Marcus, and he was not happy about missing out on getting the briefcase. He knew exactly what was in it, all about the Arcanum Disc pieces and the island it will apparently guide whoever completes it too. He had found out who I was, that we had found the first piece and that I was headed to Greenland. He knew everything."

"But how? Wait. Franklyn?"

"Yeah, Franklyn. Marcus was the one who went to Franklyn in an attempt to retrieve the briefcase, but he found out it was in my hands. He got everything from Franklyn about it, and he killed him to stop Franklyn warning me he was coming."

"That bastard!"

"While I was there, I did find a clue on a stone display that said 'a piece of the soul never leaves its true home', which I tend to read as a clue to an Arcanum Disc piece. I think it means that one of the pieces is in the Sutandan ruins, and it never left at all."

"That does make sense. But is this all worth carrying on for? People are dying, and we have opened a whole can of worms here. And this Marcus guy? He sounds dangerous; we don't need this."

"On the contrary, Franklyn entrusted us with finishing this quest for him. He has died for it, and I think we owe it to him to see it through."

Thomas stepped back for a moment deep in thought, clearly torn.

"And Marcus has seen the same clue that I have, so I think if we are serious about this, we need to get to those ruins and take a look."

"You are right. Franklyn wouldn't have given this to us if he knew we would give up. He gave his life for this, the least we can do is honour that. Shall I contact Samuel?"

"I think that would be great; it will be nice to see him."

"Okay, I will make a call."

As Thomas briefly walked off with his phone, Arthur felt a slight but strong tinge of guilt. He had left out the most important part of the story that he had found another piece of the Arcanum Disc. The reason he held this back, for now, was because after seeing what Marcus did and his ruthlessness that he didn't want Thomas to be in any more danger than he needed to be in. For now, at least, he planned to keep it to himself, and if they found the final piece, he would tell Thomas everything.

A few days later, Thomas, Samuel and Arthur were in Peru. It was a hot sunny day, and it made the bumpy ride in the 4X4 a little more uncomfortable. It didn't have a roof, so one would assume the added breeze would remove the humidity, but it only reduced it a little. Samuel had hired a 4X4 from a local town, as the main ruins from the city of Sutanda were far inland from the coast, so it was the only way. They were currently a mile or so from where they planned to leave the 4X4 and continue on foot, as the city ruin was on a slight hill, inaccessible by vehicle.

"It's so damn hot," exclaimed Arthur, putting his hands through his hair and wiping back a tiny amount of sweat from his forehead.

"Well, it is the summer in Peru, what were you expecting?" Thomas joked.

"I have just recently come back from Greenland you know, where it's kind of cold."

"Alright, make up whatever excuse you like," laughed Thomas.

"Hopefully, we will get some much-needed shade in a moment. We aren't far from the forest that surrounds this place. I checked a few maps, and the treeline is around 50 metres or so," informed Samuel.

"That coupled with the incline of the hill, it is going to be a little bit of a hike," added Arthur.

"So, where in this great ruin do you think this treasure, if it even exists, is going to be? It isn't as if other people haven't been here before," asked Samuel.

"Well, the text in the cave, which I think could be a clue, said a piece of the soul never leaves its home. Given the context, I see that as meaning a part of the Arcanum Disc never left the city. In fact, being quite well versed with the history of this place now, I would say it means it is still in what were the governmental halls."

"How on earth are we going to know what that is? It is hardly going to be signposted in an ancient collection of crumbled structures," said Samuel.

"The monarchy of the time also formed the government and advised on how the empire was run. To me, it makes sense that the palace ruins that are at the centre of the city would be where it was stored. It's just a hunch, anyway."

"Well, a hunch is better than nothing. I will be interested to see what we find," Thomas added.

"Okay, we are here," announced Samuel, pulling the 4X4 to the side of the road.

"Gather what you need, it's going to be a little bit of a hike from here on out," advised Arthur, grabbing his bag from the boot of the vehicle. He was joined by Thomas and Samuel, with Samuel only taking a flask of water.

"That it?" asked Thomas.

"You don't need anything else other than a keen mind when checking these places out, but a bit of water in the midday sun never goes a miss."

"Come on, let's get going," Arthur said, leading ahead on the trail.

The three men began the walk up a very thin stone pathway, which led the incline up the hillside. They soon entered the woodland and, although still very bright it gave some shelter from the heat. Hiking up through this area, Samuel grew curious about the story of the fall of Sutanda.

"So, give us a quick recap Arthur. What happened here?"

"You mean the city?"

"Yeah, more specifically the way it fell to the enemy."

"In a nutshell, its main rival Mahindra attacked via the ocean after a victory over one of the islands within the Sutandan Empire. Due to the distance the city had from the coast, word got back to the city that an attack was imminent. As the men pushed their way through these very trees and into the city, the Sutandan King had time to prepare a minimal defence; however, it wasn't enough. The city fell, and the King was killed."

"It's one gripping power struggle coming to an end right?"

"Not exactly as not long after the Mahendran's had conquered, a civil war broke out with the remaining citizens of Sutanda, who refused to bow to the new ruler. They managed to fight back and defeat them, taking back control of the city."

"What happened after that? Did they get back to their former glory?" Samuel asked.

"Far from it, as without a ruler and with a large portion of the upper class gone, they had no experience with running a whole civilisation. It wasn't long before weakness overcame them, and the city disbanded, with people leaving for other settlements. The Mayan people, with whom they were allied, generally accepted anyone that travelled as they came with skills that benefited them. As a result, the city became deserted and the subsequent ruin it is today came to be."

"Fascinating, I am genuinely curious as to what this place will look like. Even if we don't find what we are looking for, this place is sure to astound me."

Thomas, who walked slightly ahead, stopped in his tracks and looked back and smiled.

"Wonder no more. Guys, you are going to want to see this."

Everyone walked to Thomas and looked over in awe. They had reached the edge of the treeline and were at a level that gave a wonderful view of the ruins. Looking forward, they could see a large set of ruined structures, some overgrown by the surrounding woodland.

There were a large number of smaller buildings with missing roofs that are likely to have been where inhabitants lived, various stone paths going between the ruins as well as a large open space, which appeared to be some sort of coliseum structure. Beyond this was the outline of a much larger building, which appeared to be the ruins of a palace, which still had a roof and various faded patterns adorning its front.

"Incredible," said Samuel, looking forward with the awe of a child discovering a new toy.

"That over there is what we should head for, the large structure with the fancy roof. That looks to me to be the palace, what remains of it anyway. Seems a safe bet if the Arcanum Disc is anywhere, it is going to be in there."

"Okay, let's head for it," agreed Thomas.

They walked down a grassy embankment and began moving through one of the many routes, which would have at one time been a busy street. There was no way of knowing if this was a residential or a commercial area as the structures were so worn away it was hard to distinguish between them, but it was fascinating nonetheless. The structure and layout were like a hybrid of Mayan ruins in Mexico and Machu Picchu, which was high up in the Peru Mountains.

"I am surprised that none of the local tribes has ever repopulated this place," remarked Samuel.

"I imagine there is a great respect for what was, and the age of the ruins here could be an imposing lesson as to what has come before them," Arthur replied.

Thomas had walked ahead slightly and was out of the conversation, but he suddenly turned with a serious expression on his face, gesturing for them to come over to him quietly. Arthur and Samuel came up beside him, and they crouched by a wall. Thomas gestured ahead of them, and they looked over slightly, peaking at what was ahead.

"Man, this could take ages, this is what remains of an entire city," a man could be heard saying to another.

"I know, but I trust he knows what he is doing. I haven't seen such determination come from one man in a long time, he's almost possessed by finding this artefact."

"Why? He has never let on to me what he actually wants it for."

"It isn't the artefact he actually wants, but what it is alleged to give the beholder."

"And that being what exactly?"

"It apparently gives the location of an island, which was part of this empire that we stand within now. This island is rumoured to have vast treasures and wealth that the King moved there to spread his country's power. People have been looking for it for hundreds, if not thousands of years, and Marcus thinks he is close."

"Fair enough. Well, we have guarded enough of these expeditions of his, he had better pay up!"

Arthur watched through a crack in the wall as the two men, who were armed with automatic rifles, walked away from each other. They were walking around the outside of the coliseum.

"Damn, it looks like Marcus is already here. It makes sense, he saw the same clue, but I didn't think he would beat us here."

"It doesn't mean he has found anything; we need to keep going and get to that palace as soon as possible," said Thomas.

"Right, we need to quietly move between these structures a few at a time, keeping an eye out. Although we have seen a few over there, they could be spread all about," advised Samuel.

"Okay, on me," Arthur responded, moving off the wall and in the direction of the palace, away from the coliseum.

A few minutes later, they had moved around twenty-five metres closer to the palace, and it was not far at all. They could probably dash across but knew it would be a risky move. They were propped up against the edge of a lower wall, and Arthur looked around and immediately got himself back into cover frantically. An armed man was walking towards them and was almost within touching distance.

The man stopped and lowered his weapon, reaching for a cigarette. He lit it and stood still, with the smoke coming over the wall and over the three men. Samuel struggled to hold in a cough, but Arthur gave him a strong look of concern, shaking his head slowly. The man turned and began to walk off, and Arthur signalled to a structure opposite them to move for. He stuck his hand up and gestured to three before they all moved quickly but quietly across to the other side. Arthur went back against the wall and looked back to see they had not been spotted.

"Guys, I think we are…" he quietly said, turning to see two men, both holding weapons up to Thomas and Samuel. "…fine. Shit."

He put his hands up in the air and was gestured by the men to stand up.

"Erm, hi, guys. So, I know we just met and all, but I'm going to need you to pretend you didn't see us and let us go," Arthur said.

"Shut up," one of the men said, with the other reaching for his radio.

"Sir, we have intruders. One of them matches the description of the man you told us to keep an eye out for. What do you want us to do?"

A few moments of silence passed before a familiar voice to Arthur crackled through.

"Excellent, bring them to me. I will meet you at the coliseum area. And bring them to me alive."

"Yes, sir. You heard the man, move!" the other armed man ordered, gesturing his weapon forward.

Arthur felt a huge wave of concern wash over him as he headed against his will towards another confrontation with Marcus. He looked up, and as he entered the fairly large open space, he saw there were ten more armed guards watching him walk over.

"Stop right here and get on your knees," a guard ordered.

"What already? Not even a nice dinner first?" joked Arthur.

"Shut up!" a second guard said, pushing him to the ground. Thomas and Samuel followed him, and all three of them got down on their knees with their hands above their heads. One of the armed guards took away Arthur's handgun and threw it to the ground in front of them. Arthur breathed out in a disappointed sigh and looked up to see Marcus. He was slowly walking towards them, with a twisted smile on his face.

"Mr King! Mr Arthur King! I can't tell you how good it is to see you again so soon!" he said, with a menacingly slow speed of delivery.

"I was hoping I had frozen you out of the race, so to speak."

"Always the comedian I see, always the comedian. I admire that, I really do," Marcus said, turning to his guards, who had circled the area creating a small audience.

"Now, as you can see, my men and I have travelled a long way to find the Arcanum Disc piece that we believe is here from that clue. And it seems you have done the same, and I like that. It means I am on the right track. But see, the thing is, and this is why I am glad you are here, if I find that piece, heck, when I find that piece, that still leaves both of us at each other's heads doesn't it? And do you know why? I will tell you. It is because you have one piece, and I have one piece. You need all three pieces together to complete the puzzle, so I am going to ask again as I did in Greenland. Where is it, Arthur? Where is that piece?"

"I am never going to tell you. You will never get your hands on it. Not after what you did to Franklyn!"

"Oh, still torn up are we? Listen here; let's not allow our emotions to get in the way of what we both want so how about this. If you tell me where it is, I will let you come along and see it for yourself. How about that Arthur?"

"Shut up. I am never going to give you that piece."

"Fine, then I am going to beat it out of your sorry ass. You! Bring him to me," Marcus ordered the man behind Arthur, who picked him up and threw him towards Marcus, who punched him hard in the face. Arthur looked up, enraged and began to fight back, with the two trading blows. Arthur however, had a lot of his attacks blocked, and each time Marcus hit back and hit hard.

It didn't take long for Arthur to be knocked back by Marcus' strength, and he fell backwards, blood dripping down his face. Marcus walked over and grabbed him by the throat, holding him up.

"Now, listen to me. I don't want to get personal here. I am trying my best to be reasonable. You see, for as much of a pain in the neck you have been for, I oddly respect you. But business comes first, and I want that Arcanum Disc artefact. I have asked nicely, and even after this, you won't give in. So I wonder, what is your breaking point?"

Arthur spat on the ground next to Marcus, in a show of defiance before returning his gaze directly into his eyes.

"You obviously don't care if anything happens to you. You can't hurt a man who doesn't fear death, no. It will need to be something close, close to your heart that would hurt. How about your beloved daughter Olivia?"

Arthur looked stunned at the fact he knew about Olivia, and couldn't hide it in his expression.

"Yes, that would hurt wouldn't it Arthur. So here is how this is going to play out. If you don't tell me where what you stole from me is right now, I am going to pay your daughter a visit and will make her life a living hell until you do, do you understand?"

"If you ever go near my family, I will…"

"You'll what, kill me? You are in no position to make any threats to me Arthur, none whatsoever."

Marcus hit Arthur across the face with his fist and as he did, Thomas got up and lunged for Marcus. He got one punch to Marcus before an armed guard wrestled him back to where he was and forced him back on his knees.

"I tell you what Arthur, this guy has changed my mind right there. For that, he is now a direct deal breaker. If you don't give me the location right now, I will blow his brains out, do you understand?" Marcus snarled in Arthur's face, drawing his handgun and jamming it into Thomas' forehead. "DO I MAKE MYSELF CLEAR? FIVE! FOUR! THREE! TWO!"

"Close your eyes, NOW!" Arthur shouted at Thomas and Samuel before releasing the pin from a stun grenade and throwing it in front of Marcus. Marcus didn't have any time to react other than look down as the grenade made a pop and released a bright light. Although it was a sunny and bright day, the flash was still enough to blind for a moment and during the disorientation, Arthur, Thomas and Samuel got up and made a run for the palace. A hail of gunfire erupted around them, hitting the surrounding ruins as they ran as fast as they could. Some of the armed men had already flanked one side and there were too many of them converging on the palace location.

"I will lure them away from here, head back towards the 4X4. I have a couple of weapons stashed in the boot I could really do with having right now!" shouted Samuel.

"No, we can't split now!" Thomas replied.

"You need to get in that palace and if we all go in there, there will be too many of them. I will radio you once I am clear!" he shouted before running off.

"Ballsy bastard!" Thomas said under his breath as they ran along the side of the palace. They didn't enter and darted towards the buildings alongside it, to give the illusion that they were heading away from it. They intended to circle back as if they entered with all the men in pursuit it would be game over.

After running for what felt like an eternity of ducking and diving through various buildings, the path turned sharply and the two men were met with an opening in a rock face. Through the gap, they could see the top of a small flight of stone steps that led down into the darkness. Knowing time was not a luxury, they had to act fast.

"So, do you think this is the way into the palace?" Thomas remarked.

"There is only one way to find out," replied Arthur, gesturing for him to go ahead. "And right now, we need to hide, so either way, let's go."

Thomas gave a smile and then turned, leading the way into the unknown. After several steps down a small drop of about a metre and a half breaks the steps in two. It was here both men flattened their backs against the rocky interior and waited silently, hoping the pursuers didn't follow them. A tense moment of silence began but was interrupted by the sound of two men running just beyond the gap in the rocks.

"Did you see where they went?" a deep male voice of one of the armed guards asked.

"No. Damn it. Marcus is going to be pissed at us; how could we have lost them that easily?"

"We can't blame that damn flash bang blinding us, not now."

Arthur felt his heart pounding through his chest as he knew they were mere metres from the men. He looked over at Thomas who had begun to slowly move back. As he did, he knocked a small rock that began to knock and crash its way down the flight of stairs. It seemed amplified to their ears as the men outside reacted. All that crossed Arthur's mind was game over as he became extremely tense.

"What was that?" one of the men muttered to themselves before heading over, weapon drawn forward.

Arthur felt a bead of sweat drip down his face as he tried to remain as silent as possible. The man's shadow cast itself on the inside of the opening they were hiding in and stayed there like a spectre, all too long for Arthur's liking. It moved to suggest the man was entering the gap when the other man shouted to him.

"Over here. There is a path that looks like it is where they went. Let's check it out."

"Okay," the other man replied, taking one last look towards the gap in the rocks before following the other man on a path that led away from Arthur and Thomas. Arthur took a moment and breathed a sigh of relief.

"There is a break in the steps here with a small drop so be careful," Thomas advised very quietly in a faint whisper.

At the bottom of the steps, they walked into a larger entrance hall, which was bare. All that they saw was a doorway in front of them. It was adorned with a crumbled and faded pair of stone guards, with a weapon on each of its respective far sides.

"This looks to be the way," Thomas said, pointing forward.

Walking through the doorway, they entered a room of similar width but slightly longer. The natural light faded and from there on in darkness hid the room.

"It is a little dark in here, best put the torches on," Arthur advised.

The two lit up their torches and the darkness retreated to reveal that the room had eight large stone coffins, with four on each side set in perfect symmetry. The walls were covered in symbols that dated back thousands of years and it appeared to be a mass burial chamber.

"Judging by the site that we are under, these would appear to be the resting places of the founding fathers of Sutanda," Arthur remarked.

"The details of the engravings are incredible. Not since Egyptian burial chambers have I seen anything so beautifully crafted," Thomas responded.

"And look there, just ahead. Judging by the engravings through there could be the resting place of the guy who supposedly guards over the civilisation from the otherworld."

They both entered through the open doorway and entered a vast burial chamber. Ahead they saw a large stone coffin with a great stone impression on the wall above. On it were clear depictions of people kneeling and praying at the feet of a larger piece depicting a King.

"This must be it, the Tomb of Isirus," said Arthur.

"The founding father of the empire?"

"Yes. He was the first ruler of Sutanda, and it makes sense that he was entrusted from the grave to hide a piece of the Arcanum Disc."

"Which when all shards are together shows the beholder the location of the lost island Arcanum?"

"Exactly."

"So essentially we have been set on a treasure hunt by Franklyn, that if successful leads to another treasure hunt, fantastic. Patience really is a virtue for this one."

They both looked around the various artefacts and small treasures surrounding the coffin but couldn't see what they were looking for.

"It won't be on display will it, if it is even here?" said Thomas.

"No, I imagine we are going to have to get this open," Arthur replied as he gestured towards the lid of the coffin.

"It was never going to be easy now, was it?"

"It looks like the top isn't secured, and if we push it, it may come open."

"Okay, let's give it a shot."

They both began to push and the top portion of the coffin came up to reveal the remains of a human body, neatly positioned within the interior. They placed the stone lid on the floor and took a look inside.

"There's…nothing here," said Arthur, disheartened.

"What?"

"No treasures, no Arcanum Disc. It's just the remains of one of the Kings."

"Damn! I was counting on this. That money could come in real handy right now!"

"Surely you didn't come all this way completely for the money Thomas?"

"Not completely, the artefacts are amazing, but still…"

"And I thought my charming personality was enough to bring you along for the ride."

Arthur examined the large stone coffin once more and noticed something he had neglected to check.

"Wait a minute."

Arthur ran his hands under the coffin and felt a hidden recess. He looked underneath and could see something glisten, baiting him for a closer look. He shined his torch and saw the handle of a golden object. He pulled it and the object came loose.

"No way…Thomas, look at this!"

"What is it?"

"It's…a piece of the Arcanum Disc!"

Arthur handed it over to Thomas who examined the object. A huge smile spread across his face. As he looked it over, Arthur wandered towards the entrance to the Tomb.

"Now this has lightened my mood! People have been searching thousands of years for the Arcanum Disc and I am holding one of the pieces in my own hands! How many more do we need to find, just the one bi…"

He turned to Arthur and can see that his joyful expression had been replaced with one of grave concern.

"They have found us," Arthur said softly.

"What? How?"

"Ssshh. Come here."

Arthur beckoned Thomas over to him, and they both crouched behind a little wall that was just in from the entrance to the tomb they were in.

"It's him. He's here," said Arthur.

"I thought we had…?"

"I know."

They both peeked over the wall and saw multiple armed men slowly and methodically searching the tombs. They were armed with assault rifles and shotguns.

"We need to get out of here, quickly and quietly. We don't want them getting their hands on what we have found. We have been through too much for that," stated Arthur.

"Okay."

"On me. Let's go."

They both peeked over and saw the nearest man had turned away, so they had an opening to leave the room. They did so slowly, hugging the walls for cover as they entered the burial room. They changed position and dashed over to another piece to use as cover, this time being one of the large stone coffins. This was by a high pillar reaching to the ceiling, which provided standing cover for them one at a time. Backs to the wall, they looked up and saw that just on the other side of the wall they were up against were two armed men, almost within touching distance.

"That other route was a dead end so they must have come down here," an armed male said to another.

"It's a dead end down here. They won't have any way of escaping," the other replied.

One of the men wandered around the wall and right to the stone pillar where Arthur was crouched. Arthur moved his hand to the grip of his handgun, ready for the worst. He knew that if he had to use it, their cover was blown. Just as Arthur was about to come into the man's field of vision, someone shouted to him.

'Hey, over here! This tomb has been searched and the coffin is open. They were here, I'm sure of it!' an armed guard shouted from where they just were.

'Come on, let's go take a look' another said to the man nearest Arthur and Thomas.

The nearest man turned and headed off to where they had just found the Arcanum Disc, and Arthur let go of his gun and breathed a brief sigh of relief. He signalled to Thomas to move onwards.

They reached a break in the wall and needed to move to the next stone wall, a few metres ahead. An armed man was walking towards them and would see if they moved. Arthur pointed towards an opening to the right of where they were and gestured to move. They reached the cover position and checked to the left of the pillar. They hadn't been seen. Arthur then broke cover and moved ahead and immediately and rather, unfortunately, came face to face with an armed male.

"Hi…" Thomas spluttered in shock.

Caught by surprise, both the armed man and Arthur briefly hesitated before Arthur punched him and attempted to take him down quietly. However, the man discharged a few rounds from his weapon, drawing the attention of the other men. Arthur knocked the man out as the other armed men began to audibly move on their location.

"So much for not drawing any attention to ourselves!" shouted Thomas.

"I have always favoured plan B as an option, you should know that after all these years Thomas!" quipped Arthur.

They both ran ahead a few feet before a hail of gunfire from behind them erupted, with pieces of stone being ripped from the ancient structure that surrounded them. They dived behind cover and looked back to see there were five armed men engaging them in a firefight.

"And there was me thinking this was going to be easy," Arthur shouted over to Thomas as he drew his handgun and returned fire. Thomas followed his lead and a gun battle briefly raged, with the chamber as well as the attacking men being ripped apart.

Soon silence fell, and they appeared to have taken the initial wave of men out. Thomas gestured to Arthur to move up towards the entrance and Arthur nodded in agreement. As Thomas began to leave cover, a large blast hit the wall and knocked Thomas back. Arthur looked over and saw a heavily armoured man with a shotgun slowly advancing on them firing devastating rounds into the stone cover.

With each blast, the wall crumbled and fell away and Thomas moved further and further back towards the end. Soon, there was only a small amount of cover left and one more blast would expose Thomas to the shots. Arthur knew he had only one shot at stopping this.

He moved to his right and began to go around the shooter. Soon he was at the end of the room near the tomb entrance and took aim at the back of the armed man. He began firing and emptied several bullets into his back. One more shotgun blast sounded out, which hit the ceiling as the man fell to the ground.

"Thanks," Thomas shouted. "But I had him on the ropes," he said with a smile.

"Come on, let's get up the stairs."

They moved on and reached the foot of the stairs when three more men at the top began firing automatic weapons towards them. Arthur and Thomas both hid behind a pillar each either side of the foot of the stone steps. They took out one of the men who fell down the steps and landed just past them. They returned fire on the others when Arthur's gun clicked and ran out of bullets.

"I'm out!" Arthur shouted to Thomas.

"One second!"

Thomas fired a few more rounds before reaching into his pocket for a magazine.

"Behind you!" Arthur shouted.

A masked man grabbed Thomas and began to strangle him from behind. Thomas got out of it and the two became embroiled in a fist fight and began a violent struggle. Thomas checked the men advancing on them and heard one of them reload. He saw the assault rifle of the man who fell past them so rolled forward and picked it up. He hit the man attacking Thomas over the head and then pushed him to the ground, knocking him out.

"Thanks. That's two I owe you," Thomas said.

"Don't thank me yet!"

They resumed fire on the remaining men, and they quickly took them out. As the last bullet shells hit the floor, the silence was resumed.

"I think that is all of them," stated Arthur.

"Come on, let's get out of here. We better find that damn island after all this."

"We have all we need, trust me."

They ran up the stairs and into the entrance hall. Arthur was slightly ahead of Thomas and as he reached the foot of the steps he heard a struggle. He turned to see Thomas being held at gunpoint by the man they thought they had finally given the slip.

"Put it down," Marcus ordered, gesturing towards the gun in Arthur's hand. The man had marks and a little blood on his face, evidence of the fist fight prior to this. Arthur saw he had landed a few more blows than he thought, and felt good about it.

"You wouldn't dare," Arthur said in reference to Marcus firing his weapon at either of them.

"Don't test me, Arthur. Put your guns down now, or your friend dies. I wasn't bluffing last time, and I certainly am not now."

"Okay, okay. Nothing flash this time."

Arthur placed his handgun down in front of him and walked back a few paces while raising his hands for a few moments to show he was complying.

"What do you want Marcus?"

"Don't play me for a fool Arthur. You know exactly why we are all here, the Arcanum Disc. It is the key to that island and all of its lost treasure. You know that I am not going to let you, the daring thief masquerading as an archaeologist, get hold of it."

"And what makes you think that we have it? There was nothing down there."

"Enough. We have both been following the same clues and you just happened to get here first. I have seen the tomb you raided back there. It was the Tomb of Isirus, who was one of the forefathers of Sutanda and was entrusted with hiding the Arcanum Disc."

"Now that is just a legend, there was nothing there…"

A flash of annoyance came over Marcus, and he fired one round of his handgun up in the air and immediately pushed it back against Thomas' face. Thomas winced at the hot barrel as Marcus clicked back the hammer ready for another shot.

"Enough! Give me what you have found or I will shoot him and then you. After which I will take it from your body while it is still warm. So you can either give me the shard and walk away with your life, or lose your life and I will take it from you. Either way, you lose."

"Fine."

Arthur slowly reached for his bag and removed it from his shoulders. He took a few steps forward and placed it in the middle of the room.

"In there, all you need to do is reach in and take it."

"I am not stupid, show it to me yourself!"

"Cutting straight to the chase eh? Something you have never been good at."

"Shut up!"

Arthur opened the bag and slowly pulled out the Arcanum Disc piece. Its golden edge shined in the light as Arthur pulled it out and gestured towards Marcus.

"Now let him go."

"No. Give me the shard first."

Arthur placed the shard on the floor and took a few steps back. This had a brief hypnotic effect on Marcus as it was placed on the ground.

"Fine, it's yours. Now, who's the thief?"

"Very good Arthur, very good. Cheeky as ever I see."

Arthur stepped away several paces, and Marcus slowly moved towards it. As he did so, he slightly loosened his grip on Thomas.

"This will help lead me to the greatness that you can only dream of."

Arthur began to laugh to himself and it had the intended effect on Marcus.

"What is so funny Mr King?" Marcus enquired as he went to pick up the shard. As he did so, he had only one arm on Thomas and Arthur took his chance. He opened fire on Marcus and a few bullets connected. As the shock hit Marcus, he returned fire quicker than Arthur expected and a few bullets came right back towards him.

As Marcus was hit, he let go of Thomas who grabbed a weapon from the ground and emptied the remaining bullets of its clip into Marcus who fell to the ground, with his hand letting go of the shard. As the room fell into an eerie silence, Thomas looked up towards Arthur who was looking down at his stomach. Blood began to soak through his top, and he collapsed to the ground. Marcus lifted his head off the ground, smiling before falling back, lifeless.

"ARTHUR!" Thomas shouted.

He ran over to Arthur, who had slumped back against a pillar.

"Don't worry, it's just…a flesh wound," Arthur said as he coughed up a bit of blood. He smiled at Thomas as if trying to convince himself more than Thomas that nothing was wrong before more blood came out. "We had a good run didn't we old friend."

"Don't talk crap, Arthur. We have survived worse than this, and we always come out on top. There is no reason why that won't be the case again."

"Keep the shards away from his kind, at all costs."

"I don't care about that, you're badly wounded. We need to get you patched up and out of here now!"

Thomas reached into his backpack and got out a medical kit to try and stop the bleeding. Arthur put his hand on Thomas and gestured to him to stop, as he knew it was futile.

"I have bullets in my lungs, Thomas; I can feel it. There is no stopping the bleeding. Please look after Olivia. I don't want any of this to ever to come back on her."

"But."

"And tell her that I love her."

Thomas began to feel the inevitability of the situation but didn't stop attempting to patch him up.

"You can tell her yourself Arthur," as he looked him directly in the eyes. "You are not dying on me."

"You have always been there for me, and I cannot thank you enough. Please give me your word that you will watch over Olivia and keep her safe."

"Of course, you have my word," promised Thomas.

"This…this was the third."

"What?" Thomas replied, confused. "Third what?"

Arthur went to speak again before coughing up a large amount of blood. He looked towards Thomas before briefly shaking. Thomas looked into his eyes as Arthur's soul drained from his body.

'Arthur?'

The hall became deathly silent as Thomas realised Arthur had just died right in front of him. His eyes began to well up and a few tears fell down his face as the realisation he had gone crashed down on him. He kept asking himself why it had to end like that as he put his arms around Arthur and began to sob.

Chapter Nine

Thomas walked up to the front door of Arthur's home. He looked down, full of emotion, knowing that this was the first time he was going to lay eyes on Arthur's daughter since she found out her dad wouldn't be coming home. He composed himself before grabbing the door handle. As he did, it moved down and the door opened.

Martha looked directly into his eyes for a moment before giving him a close hug. She put her hand on his cheek for comfort and gave a half-smile through slightly teary eyes.

"Does she know?" Thomas asked.

"I have told her Arthur has died. I haven't told her how or any details other than what she needs to know," Martha replied.

"Thank you."

"She does know he was with you when he died, so she may ask a few questions."

"Okay," Thomas said quietly before moving into the front hallway. He looked up to the stairs and Olivia was standing halfway down, one arm on the handrail staring down at Thomas and Martha. She was just eleven years old but was taking in what had happened as much as anyone else.

She ran down the stairs and Thomas knelt down as she reached him. She immediately grabbed him with a tearful hug.

"I miss him so much Uncle Thomas," Olivia cried, sobbing into his shoulder.

"Me too Olivia, me too," Thomas replied as the emotion started to get the better of him.

He looked up and saw Martha weakly smile at him before a man in a smart suit walked out from a room at the end of the hall. Thomas recognised him as Martin Coakes, the solicitor that had worked closely with Arthur over the last few years. Thomas stood up and headed over and shook his hand.

"I'm sorry for your loss Mr Moyes," said Martin as he let go of his hand and held it out towards the room he just came from.

"Thank you, Martin, your thoughts are very much appreciated," Thomas replied.

Both men entered the downstairs office and sat down at a table littered with legal documents and other paperwork associated with the King estate.

"My deepest thoughts and condolences are with you and Olivia at this difficult time. I cannot begin to imagine how difficult this is for you both. As I am sure you are aware, there are a lot of things to sort out, and I thought it would be best to get things going as soon as possible, if only for Olivia's sake."

"Of course," agreed Thomas.

"Okay. According to the will of Arthur King, the house and grounds are to be left entirely to Olivia, as well as the remaining financial funds. However, this is to be locked from her until she reaches eighteen. Until such a time, as her godfather, you have been nominated to become Olivia's guardian. You don't have to commit to this, but if you do, there is financial support put by to help care for her. Alongside the aforementioned, there is a percentage of wealth solely in place for you."

"I promised Arthur as he died I would look after her, so I am happy to take her into my care, as long as she needs it."

"Excellent. Then I shall put the arrangements into place for you. Everything is taken care of legally, so you will have nothing to worry about."

"And the funeral?"

"Yes, that is to be a week tomorrow. It will be at the same place Mrs King is buried, as his wish was to be beside his late wife."

"That sounds ideal. I will inform everyone that needs to be."

"Okay. I will be in touch with regard to what we discussed. The legal side of taking guardianship shouldn't take long."

"I am more than happy to take care of her from now on if that is what Olivia would be okay with."

"She is. Martha has already had a discussion with her, and she is happy, given the circumstance."

Both men stood up and shook hands before Thomas showed him out the room. They entered the main hallway and Martin said goodbye to Olivia and Martha before leaving through the front door. Together they all stood in the doorway and watched Martin get into his car and drive away. As he disappeared from view, they closed the door and went inside.

A crack of a rifle fire shattered the silence as a one-gun salute was fired into the sky above. Thomas looked up as this happened while Olivia kept her eyes firmly on the grave of her father. The earth that will keep him for eternity was slowly placed over the coffin by two men and as it vanished from view, Olivia turned and hugged Thomas.

As mourners began to leave, Olivia received a single red rose from Martha. Taking it, she headed over to the freshly covered grave and placed it down by the headstone. She touched it with one hand before standing and looking down upon it. A tear rolled down her face as her eyes began to well up with the emotion.

"I love you Dad," she said.

She turned and headed back to Thomas and Martha, and they all went back to the car.

"You were very strong today Olivia, your father would have been so proud of you," Thomas told Olivia.

"Thanks," she replied half-heartedly.

Olivia sat in her seat and Thomas smiled before closing the door. Moments later the car engine ignited and the car began to move off.

"She hasn't said much today, I really hope she is going to be okay," Thomas said with concern, as he looked at Olivia through the interior mirror.

"It has hit her hard. Heavens, what am I saying? It has hit us all hard. But we will stay close by her and give her all the support she needs. She will be okay, but it will take time," Martha said.

"I hope you are right," Thomas replied as he took his eyes off her and took in the oncoming road.

Olivia blankly looked out of the window as the scenery started to move by at a faster rate, and she began to drift off into a deep sleep.

A rumble of thunder came through the window and disturbed Olivia. She opened her eyes and checked the time, and realised she had been asleep for a couple of hours. She sat up and rubbed her eyes, adjusting to the room before picking up the newspaper that had fallen on the floor, turning it face up to see the headline. It was the local press and it read 'Ten years on—Arthur King remembered'.

A photo of Arthur on a mountain top was below the headline and was a fond one to Olivia. Olivia was now twenty-one and a recent graduate of the University that Arthur lectured at alongside his adventures around the world. Arthur had taught for a few years after his military service along with many years of more action-packed activities tracking down rare treasures for people who would pay highly.

She placed the newspaper down and stood from the sofa, leaving the room and moving into the main hallway. Heading up the wooden staircase she looked briefly behind her and saw the sun coming through the window, striking an elegant shadow across the wall. Olivia reached the top and walked towards her bedroom, stopping as she passed Arthur's old study. She hadn't been in there in quite some time, but today felt right and would make her feel closer to him. She placed her hand on the door handle and pushed it down.

The door swung open revealing a relatively small study. At the centre of the room was a large wooden desk with books and paperwork strewn across. To her left, Olivia saw a large bookcase, and besides that, there were a few pieces of art hanging.

Olivia headed over to the desk and began looking over the paperwork that was scattered across it. Moving a few documents, she noticed a book nestled underneath and recognised it immediately.

She sat down and brought it towards her, reading the title *Atlantis—The Legend of the Lost City*. She smiled, remembering being told this story countless times as a child. She flicked open the book and began looking over the pages and remembered asking her father if such a mysterious place could exist hidden away from the world. She closed her eyes and fondly recounted such a time she was read this as a bedtime story.

'Daddy, can you take me here one day?' Olivia asked.

'Sadly Atlantis isn't real, it's just for stories' Arthur replied. *Seeing Olivia become immediately disappointed, however, made him change his tone.* *'However, I am convinced that there are places just like it, out there waiting to be discovered.'*

'Like where, what places?'

'Well I can let you in on a little secret but only if you promise not to tell anyone. Can you do that?'

'I promise.'

'Pinkie swear?'

Arthur raised his hand to Olivia, and they linked little fingers.

'Pinkie swear.'

'Okay. I believe that there is a beautiful island out there waiting to be discovered. It was part of a King's great and powerful empire thousands of years ago. Now, the King had some enemies, and they wanted to take away that power, and they found he had an island hidden away and attacked it. After this, they came to the King's home, and they had a great fight.

He lost, and in his last moments and not knowing his island had been found, hid its location on a treasure. He ordered his loyal and most trusted Knights to split it into three and hide it in far corners of the world.'

'And no one has found it?

'No, not one person. The people who defeated the King tried to find it again but never could. They wrote stories about it that have been passed on through the ages, but it is now seen as a myth. I want to find it, and show it to the world.'

'Can I see it? It sounds amazing.'

'Of course. I am going to find it and show you true beauty. It is one of the world's greatest remaining mysteries and I fully plan on solving it.'

'And what is it called?'

'The very definition of a deep secret. Arcanum.'

Olivia smiled at the memory and decided to place the book back on the shelf nearby. She headed over to it and traced her fingers along the spines of a line of books, searching for where the book belonged. She didn't find a gap but found where the book should be alphabetically another copy in its place. Perplexed, Olivia pulled it out and looked at them both, one in each hand.

Both copies were completely identical. Olivia looked up at the gap where the book was and saw something behind. She removed a few of the nearby books and saw a message written along the wall beside a numeric pad. The message read 'The sum of two tales'.

Both confused and intrigued by its discovery, Olivia instinctively typed '2' into the numeric pad. A beep denying entry sounded. Knowing her father set this, she realised she

93

should know it wouldn't be that simple. She ran the clue through her head a few times.

Drawing up nothing, she looked down and saw the two books in her hands and had an idea. She put one copy of the book on the desk and then opened the other and turned it to the back page, reading the last page number. Maybe each copy of the book is one of the two tales that equal the number she needed? That would explain why two copies of the same book exist.

'32. 32 times two equals 64…'

Olivia input the number 64 into the numeric pad and hit enter. After a small pause, a green light displayed and a beep was heard. A sense of excitement ran through Olivia's body as a jarring noise began. A section of the bookshelf opened slightly like a door, and Olivia moved over to it. She saw a space had opened up and entered through the newly revealed doorway.

Adjusting to the old darkened room beyond the bookshelf, Olivia noticed an old torch on a small wooden shelf to her right. She picked it up and when it didn't turn on she banged it a few times before it came to life, illuminating the newly discovered surroundings. Olivia saw she was standing at the top of a short flight of steps that led down into complete darkness. She put the torch in front of her and began to slowly descend, and with each step further down she got more excited. Her father had kept a secret room in the house that she didn't know of, and her mind began racing with anticipation as to what she might find.

At the bottom of the steps, Olivia entered a small room that was a lot colder than the rest of the house. As she moved the torchlight around, Olivia saw various artefacts, maps and assorted treasures, all spoils from Arthur's expeditions and discoveries from around the world. In the centre of the room directly in line with the entrance was a large chest. Olivia was drawn to it and squatted down in front of the mysterious object.

It was covered in a thick layer of dust and clearly hadn't been touched for many years. She put the torch down on a nearby surface and kept it aimed at the chest so she could see. She found the lock and clicked it open, slowly lifting the lid open. Inside, she found two-thirds of an incomplete golden artefact, a map and various documents and research papers.

She read over some of the notes and saw a large red circle with the words Arcanum scribbled in her father's handwriting. She took a step back and realises that this was the potential location of the island she was told of as a child, along with hypothesised sets of coordinates and accompanying notes. He had kept them locked away from the world secure in this chest, but Olivia felt she was destined to find them. She picked up the artefact and stood, looking down at it with an intense desire to contact Thomas as soon as possible to see what he thought of what she had found. She turned and headed back up the steps, and began to pack a bag for a trip into London.

Chapter Ten

Olivia shuffled in her chair and looked down into her bag, checking she had everything she needed. Confirming this, her mind began to wander as she looked around the hall she was sat waiting in. Thomas was now head of his own company and had premises in the heart of London.

Olivia loved coming here when she was younger and looking along the marbled floored hall shimmering in the lights reminded her of running around with friends as a young child when she came by after school while waiting for Thomas to finish for the day. A nearby phone at the reception desk rang and this broke her concentration.

"Okay, I will send her in," Thomas' personal assistant said. "Olivia, he is ready for you now. Please, follow me."

Olivia stood and grabbed her bag before following the personal assistant down the short hall. She opened one of two mahogany doors and ushered her in. As she entered, she saw Thomas with his back turned looking out of the window. He turned and smiled. His hair was now grey, but he still had a youthful look on his face for someone in their early fifties.

"Olivia, it is so good to see you. What a lovely surprise," Thomas remarked. "That will be all Sarah, thank you," and with that, his personal assistant smiled and left, closing the door behind her. Thomas and Olivia hugged and had a kiss on the cheek.

"Please, take a seat. How are you?"

"Okay considering, thank you, how are you?" Olivia replied.

"The same as you I presume. Today is ten years since Arthur died and it still feels fresh when I think about it. I can't believe so long has passed. And you have grown so much Olivia, I know he would be so proud of how you are doing."

"Thank you."

"I was going to come by and see you tonight, which makes me wonder, what has made you come all the way into London to see me at such short notice?"

"I have found something that I feel you need to see."

"Oh? You have my attention, Olivia."

"Okay. This is going to sound a little daft but did you know of any secret rooms within my home?"

"No I didn't, but I have a feeling you have found something of that description?"

"Well, I was looking through my dad's study this morning and I discovered a passageway behind a bookshelf. This led down into a chamber I never knew existed, and inside I found a load of treasures, presumably spoils from all of his adventures."

"Wow, see I did wonder where he kept a lot of the things we found while having our little adventures around the world all those years ago."

"That is what I thought so I didn't think much of it until I found something of great interest. May I?" Olivia said as she gestured towards her bag.

"Of course, please."

Olivia reached into her bag and pulled out a package, which was covered in cloth. She placed it on the desk but didn't unfold it straight away.

"Did my father ever tell you of his belief of the existence of a place called Arcanum?"

"Of course, all of the time actually. It became his goal in his later life to locate it. Like a moth to the flame, the lure of supposed gold and treasure alongside an archaeological find that would make him famous was an irresistible combination."

"He told me about it as a child all the time as well, I loved hearing about it."

"We actually spent a while looking together and did make some great progress with piecing some of the clues together. Before his untimely passing, he told me he had made a breakthrough, but he never got to tell me what it was. When he died, I stopped looking, as it didn't feel right without him."

"His passion for it definitely left an impression on my imagination, but I thought it was just a story, just like those of Atlantis and Avalon. However, on finding these, I am led to believe otherwise."

She opened the cloth and revealed the two Arcanum Disc pieces, a map and assorted documents.

"My god," Thomas exclaimed as he took in what had been unveiled.

"This map has an area circled with some notes and coordinates, and these documents all talk of an island of mystery. I believe he had hypothesised a location of where he believed Arcanum is and was planning an expedition that never actually occurred due to his death."

"On the day he died, Arthur and I found an item that matches the two parts you have presented here today. He told me to keep it hidden away, as the world wasn't ready for the secret that it kept. He told me it was one of three pieces of a key. I wonder…"

Thomas headed towards a safe in the corner of the office. He opened it and pulled out a large package and brought it over to the table. He unfolded it and Olivia was shocked to see he had the final piece of the Arcanum Disc that she was missing.

"Amazing, you have the missing piece!"

"We found this on the day your father died. It was said to be part of the Arcanum Disc artefact that when placed together revealed the location of the place that we seek."

He placed the pieces next to each other on the table and then put them together. His face washed over with astonishment and wonder. Now complete, the artefact was a golden Disc that had ancient writing around its edge with an ancient map in its centre.

"Fascinating! I had never even thought of looking in this remote region of the world. Now that I think about it, all the clues and stories in myth all point to a place such as this."

Thomas grabbed a pen from his desk and began making additional markings on the map below the faded marks from Arthur.

"The hypothesis was so close. With the information from the Arcanum Disc, it looks to be only slightly to the south-west of what Arthur believed."

"I believe that finding this place was of such importance to my father that it was to become his legacy; however, this was sadly cut short ten years ago. I want to travel to these coordinates and see if he was right, and I want you to come with me like you would have gone with him."

Thomas sat back and looked deep in thought.

"I'm sorry Olivia. I spent almost a decade of my life exploring with your father, but since the day he died, I can't bring myself to carry it on, I have moved on. And besides, I'm afraid to say I am not as young as I used to be."

"Is there no way I can persuade you? You were at his side as he searched for this place, and I have found what could be the thing you were both looking for all those years. It would be right for you to be by my side while I carry on his quest, just this once."

"I don't know. I do like the idea of knowing once and for all if all the searching was leading to anything."

"Humanity has always pushed the boundaries of what we understand, a curiosity that gives a sense of overwhelming adventure. These hopes and dreams become the lifeblood of our species, and I believe that my dad had this deep within him. But chasing this dream killed him. Imagine having the ability to make another person's dream a reality, would you turn down such an opportunity?"

"I guess you are right. He had found the two parts of the Arcanum Disc and locked them away, and we found what is now apparent to be the final piece when he died. No wonder he was so happy when we discovered it."

"So is that a yes to coming along?"

"Yes. It looks like we are going on an adventure!"

"I was thinking getting there by boat would be best due to where it is, but I am a little inexperienced in the planning area."

"Leave that with me. I still have a friend in the shipping industry that owes me a favour. We will need to get a team together so I will try and contact some people I used to work with. Do you know anyone?"

"I know of two people who would be perfect, two friends who were on my archaeology course."

"Okay great, if you go and talk to them and see if they are interested, I will see what I can do with regard to a boat and will call you when plans are made."

Olivia smiled and began putting the items she brought with her back in her bag. Thomas helped, and he gave her a hug to say goodbye.

"See you soon," Olivia said warmly.

"Looking forward to it," Thomas replied as he held open the door. Olivia left and headed out through the lobby and into the busy city street outside. She reached for her phone and began dialling the number of her childhood friend Lauren Winters. She pressed call and brought it to her ear. After a few connecting tones rang out, a familiar voice picked up on the other end of the line.

"Hi Lauren, it's Olivia."

"Well, hello stranger, how are you doing?"

"Very well thank you. Listen, I have come across the adventure of a lifetime and was wondering if you are interested in coming along?"

"Now that is the way to get the attention of someone! I would love to hear more, what is it?" Lauren replied intrigued.

"Let's just say I have found an opportunity to find something that has been lost for thousands of years. Come by my house this afternoon and I can tell you all about it. Oh, and see if Callum is interested."

"That sounds great. Okay, I will try and get hold of him, but at the very least, I will be round this afternoon, say two o'clock?"

"Two works for me. See you soon."

"Bye!"

Olivia put the phone away and smiled, heading towards the station nearby. The day had quickly become one of those rare and unexpected days where the ending was completely unpredictable.

"Who was that?" enquired Callum, as his voice travelled from the front room into the hallway where Lauren had just hung up the call.

She walked into the front room and stood near Callum, who was sat on the sofa with his laptop looking at a collection of photographs of a villa in Majorca.

"Olivia. I haven't heard from her in a fair while, it was nice to speak to her."

"I bet. It must have been even longer since I last saw her, graduation even. How is she doing?"

"She sounded well, but we didn't actually talk much in the way of a catch-up."

"Oh?"

"Yeah, she briefly said that she had found, in her words, the adventure of a lifetime and that she wanted us both to pop by to see her at her place to find out more."

"How mysterious. She has definitely peaked my interest."

"Yeah, me too. I said I would swing by this afternoon, would you like to come along?"

"Can do. But first, get back here," he replied, putting his hand on the sofa next to him. "We have this to finish looking at."

"Regardless of what Olivia wants, this is pretty exciting."

Lauren quickly tied up her long dark into a ponytail and grabbed her glasses before sitting down to look at the screen.

"So you were saying before the phone rang, this is your parent's villa?"

"Yeah, that's the one. It has actually been in the family for many generations so it's pretty much the Holt residence over there. Seeing as we have been together for a few years now I thought it was long overdue that you got to check it out."

He showed her a photo of the villa from the front, which was quite recent, dated within the last six months or so.

"It is beautiful, the building is so nice, and those surroundings!"

"Oh yeah? Wait until you see the view it has of the sea," he boasted, handing her another photo from the rear of the property.

"You can see this from the back of the villa? That is amazing!"

"Yeah, you can see the sunset rise and set on the horizon of the sea while on the beach every day, it's truly incredible."

"Incredible? Now that is an understatement!"

"So, I think I already know the answer, but do you want to go there?"

"Yes!"

"How does next week sound?"

"What! That soon? Are you for real?"

"We are off for a few weeks already, so why not make the most of it? It's a family villa so the only arranging we need is for the flights."

Lauren hesitated for only a moment as the rush of potential fun ahead rushed through her head.

"Okay, let's make the arrangements," she agreed excitedly. She smiled and gave him a kiss, and got up and turned to leave the room, heading towards the kitchen. "I'm going to grab a coffee, do you want one?"

"Sure, yes please."

Lauren turned and headed into the kitchen with a huge smile on her face as she turned on the kettle and looked out of the window waiting for it to boil.

The fresh sea breeze was a welcome change to the city air that Thomas had unwillingly gotten used to. He had arrived at the dockyard where a long-time friend resided, and he had a favour that was owed a return, and he felt given the circumstances now was that time.

As he approached the small unit on the side of one of the docksides, Thomas walked through an open gate and looked up. The sign read 'Jones Salvage' and he knew he was at the right place, the only question was if his unannounced arrival would mean the man he was there to see would be present. Thomas reached the door to the offices and hesitated a few moments before knocking three times.

A few moments passed before a rumble of a chair scraping along the floor could be heard followed closely by footsteps coming to the door. A shadow appeared on the other side of the glass and then the door opened. He had changed, but it was still the man he remembered.

"It's been a while, Samuel."

"Thomas Moyes?"

"You look like you have just seen a ghost!"

"Come here," Samuel said as he opened his arms, with the two men embracing in a hug. Samuel was now the owner of a salvage company after his days of treasure hunting in more exotic locations were done. Thomas had loaned him the money to start a few years ago and was impressed at what he was seeing. Over the years he had gained a more rugged look, with his longer blonde hair replaced with a shorter style and a slight beard.

"It's good to see you, what brings you around these parts without even a call ahead?"

"Remember the little adventures we used to have looking for the Arcanum Disc with Arthur?"

"Do I remember? I still haven't had as much fun since then, no matter what thrills I have attempted while out salvaging the seas."

"Well, his daughter Olivia came to see me today, and she has found the final piece."

"Oh, did she? In that case, you had better come in," he smiled as he gestured for Thomas to come inside the office unit.

"I thought that might grab your attention."

Thomas entered and Samuel closed the door behind them, switching the sign over to read closed.

"Would you like a drink?"

"Please."

"If memory serves you quite like this," Samuel said as he held up a bottle of Thomas' favourite cider.

"You know me too well, yes please."

"Two glasses it is," he said as he began to pour one for each of them.

"I like what you have done with the place, looks like business is booming now."

"It is yeah, I won't bore you with the details, but we got a nice bunch of lucrative contracts from a company in China and it has made things a lot more comfortable around here. But obviously, it was your cash boost at the start of this venture of mine that got me started."

"It was and still is a pleasure. We needed something else to do after Arthur died and this seems perfect with your experience shipping."

"I couldn't agree more. I haven't forgotten what today is either, to Arthur," stated Samuel as he raised his glass.

"To Arthur," Thomas agreed as he chinked his glass with Samuel.

"So, tell me more about this find of Olivia's."

"She dropped by earlier and said she had found a secret area at the back of Arthur's study."

"Secretive so and so, doesn't surprise me."

"She said down there were dozens of treasures from his many trips and expeditions as well as a piece of the Arcanum Disc and a few assorted documents."

"So when we had our untimely last expedition together all those years ago, he had one tucked away we didn't know about?"

"Apparently so, yeah."

"Hmmm, interesting. That would explain his higher than usual excitement. I will never forget that day, what an adventure."

"I still can't believe we found a piece of the Arcanum Disc in the backyard of the Sutandan Empire, I mean fancy that it wasn't found in all those years until we stumbled across it?"

"Do you remember when we were walking through the coliseum when we came across Marcus and his team of hired morons?"

"I do, yes. Arthur insisted we sneak by, but when they saw us, we had that confrontation where he punched that bastard right in the face."

"Yeah, I remember," Samuel said with a laugh. "We had them on the ropes though didn't we!"

"We certainly did, then as one of them drew a gun we decided to leg it!"

"That's right!"

"I have never seen you move so fast right there."

"I didn't have a gun, and they all did, what else are you going to do?"

"Fair point there."

"And then we decided to split to lose them, you ran back in the 4X4's direction, and we ran on towards where we thought the Arcanum Disc was and by sheer luck from the path fleeing Marcus led us we found it."

"I guess that is the only good thing that bloke ever did for us."

"True. And we both know what happened down there in that tomb."

"Sadly so. When you made your way down to the 4X4 that evening with Arthur's body, I thought he was just wounded, so it was a huge shock to me. I thought the quest for Arcanum ended there, but you coming here leads me to believe there is something more to this story cut short that day."

"There does seem to be more to it, yes. She brought another piece of the Arcanum Disc and putting it together with the other two pieces revealed a location further south-west of where we initially guessed. Look at this," Thomas said, handing over the map with revised notes and coordinates on it.

"To my knowledge, there is nothing for hundreds and hundreds of miles in that area of ocean, not one thing."

"Which is why I am confident that as it's a little unexplored that we might get lucky."

"We?"

"Yes, *we*. Olivia and I would like you to join us in a little adventure to go and discover what is at these coordinates and to see if Arthur was right."

"You know what? Yes. One hundred per cent yes. I haven't had something this interesting come across my desk in a long time. We could use one of my ships that is in the docks not too far from here. When did you want to go?"

"As soon as you can be ready Samuel," Thomas said, with a smile spread across his face. "As soon as you can be ready."

Chapter Eleven

The doorbell echoed through the front hall and Olivia headed over and opened the door. She was greeted by Callum Holt and Lauren Winters, the latter being a close lifelong friend of Olivia. Callum was the long term partner of Lauren and had met Olivia at University. He was athletic with a messy hairstyle.

"Hey, it's great to see you both," said Olivia.

"Likewise!" Lauren replied, hugging Olivia warmly.

"Hey, Olivia, how are you doing?" enquired Callum.

"Very well thank you and yourself?"

"Enjoying time away from the office!"

"All he talks about are those damn numbers from the accounts he deals with, so thank you in advance for pulling him away from it!" Lauren exclaimed.

"And thank you for pulling her away from her training, we both needed the break! However, I feel with the nature of this visit, as nice as it is, she isn't going to get away from the topic too much!"

"Oh, the teaching training! How is it going, I thought you had finished now?"

"It is going well, I'm in the last few weeks now, and we have been given a week off. Hopefully, if it all goes well I will begin a position next month!"

"Oh, congratulations!" said Olivia joyfully.

"Thank you. So, what is this big adventure you mentioned earlier that has us so intrigued?"

Olivia smiled before ushering them to follow her through the hall and up the stairs.

"I'll show you. Follow me this way."

They walked up the stairs and reached the top. Olivia turned and saw Callum was lagging behind them a little.

"What is it?" Olivia enquired.

"This place, it is amazing. Just looking at the artwork that adorns the staircase wall is jaw-dropping. Your dad collected some incredible pieces on his travels."

"He did. I am truly blessed to have them around me. You have seen them before though right?"

"Yeah, but I haven't been here in a little while so I got a little distracted, sorry."

"Don't be sorry, it's alright!"

Callum re-joined them, and they all walked along the corridor and into Arthur's study. They walked past the now open doorway at the back of the bookshelf and descended the stairs.

"This is so cool!" Callum said excitedly.

"I was in here earlier, and I found a panel by pure chance behind that bookshelf we have just passed through. I managed to get it open and this stairwell was behind it. I came down and found something quite fascinating."

They all walked into the chamber at the bottom of the stairs and Lauren and Callum looked intrigued. They started looking around in awe, taking in all of the treasures and artefacts that had been hidden for many years.

"What is this place?" asked Lauren.

"As you know, my dad was an archaeologist and explorer who went around the world discovering hidden artefacts and lost civilisations. This room appears to be where he stored all of the things he found on his travels that he found to be extra special or of some importance."

"But why would he want to keep this stuff secret? Surely if it is of great importance it should be on public display in a museum or something?" enquired Callum.

"That is what I thought, especially as he did donate so many of his finds to the British Museum. At first, I assumed it was because of an item's value, or if he had an additional use first of all, but then I found this."

Olivia pointed to the box, which was now open, where she found the items relating to Arcanum. She had placed all of the contents on the table beside it, ready for presentation. They all gathered around and looked down on the scattered artefacts.

"Wow, what is this stuff?" said Lauren as she looked down and began to examine what Olivia had found.

"It is the reason I have brought you down here today. Have you heard of Arcanum?"

"No, I haven't heard of it before," responded Callum.

'Neither have I, what is it?' added Lauren.

"It's quite long-winded, so bear with me," Olivia said, as she proceeded to tell them of the history of the Sutandan Empire, the artefact and fabled island.

"And your dad was looking for it, this artefact and lost island?" asked Callum.

"Correct, he spent the last few years of his life searching the globe for the three pieces of the Arcanum Disc, and no one other than his crew he travelled with knew he only needed to locate one more piece of the puzzle. He believed that if he found all three pieces, then the island could be rediscovered."

"This place, the main civilisation I mean, what was it like?" enquired Lauren.

"It has been compared to great ancient civilisations like the ones that existed within the Mayan period. The rivalry and subsequent war between the two powers have been compared to those of Calakmul and Tikal."

"Tikal and Calakmul?" Callum queried, a little confused.

"I've heard of those places. In the classic period of Mayan history, they were two superpowers of that era who were in a struggle for dominance," Lauren added.

"But if this place is real and does actually exist, then why like the aforementioned places has it not been found?" said Callum.

"My dad firmly believed that an island that large could not simply vanish. When he died, he was on an expedition to find a piece of the Arcanum Disc, which was handed to his friend Thomas Moyes. However, neither he nor anyone else knew that all three pieces had been discovered, until I found this all today."

"And how do you know where this place is supposed to be if your dad spent so long searching and didn't find it?"

"I went to see Thomas today, and he had the final piece locked in a vault. We put it together and it revealed a location that was strikingly close to the notes hypothesised on this map. We are going to get a team together to sail out to this exact point and see if the island is there, and I want you to come with me."

"You can count me in, this is fascinating. Imagine, if the three of us were part of a team to rediscover a lost land like this? We would be famous!" Callum said excitedly.

"I agree. This is incredible, potentially turning myth into legend. I'm in. Besides, if we find it, I'm having first rights to teach it (she laughs). When do you want to go?"

"As soon as I hear back from Thomas, we should be ready. It will probably be a few days at most."

"Callum, I am more than happy to postpone our trip to Spain if you are? We could do this and then still have time to go after."

"Yeah, of course, it's a family villa anyway so it's free whenever. And besides who would turn down an extra adventure away?"

"Thank you, guys; I promise this will be worth it," said Olivia, happy to have them both coming along.

Five days later, arrangements were finalised. Thomas had spoken with someone who used to help supply transport for himself and Arthur, and he had arranged a small vessel to privately take them across to the coordinates they found on the map. The crew were aware of the usually over ambitious requests made of them, so were more than happy to accommodate. Olivia, Thomas, Callum and Lauren had come aboard and as the ship made its final preparations, Officer Murdoch showed them around.

"To your right is the kitchen, where our chef cooks all of our meals. You'll get a taste of his cooking later on this evening."

As Murdock smiled they all saw the head chef Sebastian walk out from the walk-in freezer carrying a small box. He gave a nod towards the new arrivals.

"And here he is!"

"Welcome aboard! I promise the food I am preparing won't make you want to jump overboard, regardless of what this one here says!"

"Yeah, yeah. Tell that to the last person who ate one of your meals!"

"Ha, trust me when I say that the only thing that would make a man want to jump overboard is this man's company!"

"Alright, alright Sebastian!" laughed Murdoch. "And down those stairs are the crew quarters, the maintenance room and our small armoury."

"Small armoury?" Olivia asked, a little surprised.

"Oh, not to worry, it's only a precaution. Where we are going there is a small risk of pirates, so this is merely a deterrent. We have never actually had to use them…yet."

Murdock gave a sly grin and then carried on moving forward.

"And finally, we have your rooms. There are three here, but I will leave the politics of who sleeps where up to you. I am going to head back up to the top deck while you settle in."

"Thank you," acknowledged Lauren.

"See you all at dinner," Murdoch responded as he headed back along the hall and walked left and out of view. The three of them checked the rooms and Lauren and Callum both went into the nearest one.

"This one is nice so we will settle in here and unpack our things," said Callum.

"Okay cool. In that case, I will take the one opposite. They don't look too bad. Speak to you in a bit."

Olivia walked in and closed the door behind her. She threw her bag down on the bed and looked out of the window at the endless miles of the sea with no differing horizon. She knew that it was going to be a long trip.

A few hours later, Olivia was stood up in front of the entire crew of the ship (who numbered around ten) and was giving a little presentation about why they were out at sea and what they were searching for. They were in a fairly small meeting room which was just off the hall from the staff canteen. A map of the world with greater oceanic details was already up, so Olivia was using this along with a few of the artefacts she'd taken over with her to see Thomas with initially.

"…and this area here is where we think this island maybe," Olivia said, ending a very familiar pitch that she had already given to Thomas, Callum and Lauren.

"I admit. I like the idea of finding a forgotten island just like the next guy, but surely in this age, we have discovered everything that was hiding at sea?" a man called Travis asked, gesturing towards the map. Samuel smiled and chimed in.

"Well, not exactly. There are places on this planet so remote that even now, aren't really seen."

"Exactly, like Tristan da Cunha and the Pitcairn Islands. Even though they have islanders, they are some of the most remote places on earth. So there is a slim chance that we may find what we are looking for," Olivia responded.

"But surely if there was an island that was once a part of a great ancient superpower, there would have been some indication of its existence? I mean all this time and nothing?" pressed Travis.

"Even if this place does exist, in all of the myths and legends the island was attacked and the islanders all but wiped out thousands of years ago. I imagine if we do find it, it will be completely deserted and nothing but a fascinating ruin," Olivia advised.

"And the coordinates that we are going towards are at a point that is outside of all shipping lanes that I know of. We are going into the unknown, and we are going alone," said Samuel.

"Well, I am all for it. It's nice to be going on a new adventure for once," added Travis.

"I will drink to that!" a fellow crew member stated smiling.

Everyone present raised a glass and smiled. Olivia joined them and then looked towards the back of the room and saw Thomas who nodded approvingly. She saw Callum slip out and head out to the rear deck, and in need of some fresh air herself she followed him out.

As the sea air met Olivia with a refreshing grasp, she looked out onto the small rear deck of the ship and saw Callum looking out to the sea they were leaving behind as the ship moved further on towards its destination.

"There you are. Am I capturing you at a rare moment of thought?" Olivia teased.

"Oh, nice one! I was just thinking about the holiday."

"Ah, the Villa in Spain you and Lauren mentioned earlier on?"

"That's the one."

"Hopefully dragging you out here isn't a worse option."

"Of course not, always good to get a little more build-up anyway."

"What do you mean, you and… Oh!"

"What?"

"It's your five-year anniversary tomorrow, isn't it?"

"Yep, five years already, time flies by."

"Maybe now is the time to ask her to be your beautiful bride? Am I right?" Olivia playfully asked.

"No comment! You are just looking for an event to help prepare."

"Well, I do know where my skills are!"

"Do you think we will honestly find this place? I mean your dad looked for almost a decade."

"Oh, nice subject change! He did, but I believe the only reason he couldn't find it is because he didn't have the missing piece that showed where it is. Now, we have it, I am very hopeful we can finish what would have been his legacy."

"Well, you have me convinced. I am going to turn in for the night, I don't know about jumping overboard, but that dinner has made me want to do one thing, sleep."

Callum turned and began to walk inside.

"Oh, and you were right a moment ago. But don't tell her!"

"I knew it! Don't worry, your secret is safe with me."

"It had better be! Goodnight."

Olivia waved Callum off and then turned and looked out towards the ocean. She smiled to herself and was full of hope as the setting sun gave the gentle waves a warming glow. After a moment of pondering, she too headed back inside and went straight to her room.

She closed her cabin door and lay down on the bed and freed herself of thought. In a short space of time, she drifted off and got a good night of sleep.

A few days passed with very little in the way of adventure, and Olivia had started to grow tired of endless ocean view with no land in sight. Looking down at her desk, she finished reading the end of another chapter of a book that she had managed to borrow from Lauren and stood up, placing it down on the shelf nearby. She left the room and headed down the hallway and climbed a small set of stairs that led to the crew area. She knocked on Samuel's Office three times and politely waited for a response. It wasn't long until his booming voice was heard from the other side.

"Come in."

Without hesitation, Olivia opened the door and entered the small but cosy office. Samuel was sat behind a desk reading a map and stood as she entered.

"Ah, Olivia, what a pleasure. How can I help?"

"I was just wondering how the search was going, and if we had reached the coordinates yet?"

"As a matter of fact yes we have. We reached them about six hours ago, but we haven't found anything yet. We are currently in the process of turning around and having a look slightly off the location to see if we have any luck."

"Has there been no indication that we are near any land whatsoever?"

"Not yet no. Usually, the sea is less calm, but it's remained the same thus far. I will keep you posted. Anything else I can help you with?"

"No, thank you."

Olivia turned down the stairs into the hallway from earlier. She saw the cabin door to Thomas' room was slightly ajar. They locked eyes, and he smiled at her.

"No luck yet I see?" Thomas asked.

"Not yet. I am not expecting to find it easily though. It took my dad all that time to track down the Arcanum Disc so this isn't going to be a walk in the park."

"Ha, now that is true."

"I have been meaning to ask, all these years actually. What happened when my dad died?"

"We were searching for a piece of the Arcanum Disc and as you can gather we found it. On our way out we were attacked by a group of rival treasure hunters, who had a few hired mercenaries with them. He died saving my life from those savages, and I am forever in his debt for that."

"What happened to them?"

"The people who attacked us? They were all killed, but I believe there are still many more groups like them still out there, hunting for the light that would guide them to the lost island and its treasure. I think that is why Arthur had kept everything tucked away in the room you discovered. Even I didn't know he had found the rest of the Arcanum Disc."

"If we ever find this place, we need to send them a postcard."

"Ha yes, the tagline of 'wish you were here' was made for that one card alone!"

She smiled and nodded once before she turned and entered her cabin. Closing the door behind her, she moved over to her bed and lay down. She began to mull over and process what she was just told about that day her father died, and got lost in thought. She soon nodded off and drifted into a deep sleep.

Chapter Twelve

A series of loud bangs punctuated through the dull rumble of the ship as it swayed quite haphazardly from side to side. Olivia woke with a start and sat up. She saw her clock indicate it was only early evening, but it had suddenly become very dark, with only a dull source of light coming into the room. Another bang was heard, this timeless fierce than the other, and it was coming from the cabin door.

"Olivia, Olivia!" Thomas could be heard shouting through the door.

Olivia went to the door and opened it, looking at Thomas and slightly confused by his sudden urgency.

"What is it?" she asked, confused.

"You are going to want to see this. Follow me."

Olivia nodded and closed the door behind her and followed him up to the bridge. When they walked in, Olivia was surprised to see that Samuel, Lauren, Callum, Travis and a few other assorted crew members were also present.

"What is going on?" asked Olivia.

"The conditions, they have changed drastically and almost instantly. It was a calm sea, but now, a fog has descended and the seas have become rough, as you can feel. This is most unusual," Samuel explained.

Olivia faded out about halfway through his answer to her question. Something had caught her eye out of the front windows of the bridge, and she couldn't look away. *What the hell is that?* She headed towards the door and headed out onto the top deck on the right side of the bridge.

"Olivia, where are you going?" asked Thomas, but she didn't hear him.

Outside, a colder wind had arrived, and alongside the grey skies and the thick fog that had appeared, it added a very eerie atmosphere to the now hidden sea. Olivia looked forward to what she saw. It was only a glimpse, but it looked like a dark object dancing in the distance. She looked back at the bridge briefly and could see Samuel looking down at his navigational system with a worried look on his face.

Thomas looked over his shoulder and saw the compass and navigation read-outs were varying wildly as if there was something interfering. Olivia walked forward to the railing and focused her vision forward into the unknown. Then, it appeared again. The fog slowly thinned out indicating a large physical presence was in the near distance and slowly a series of large rocky land masses came into view. The ship was heading straight for them, and Olivia realised that her heartbeat began to pick up.

"ROCKS! THERE ARE ROCKS AHEAD!" she shouted towards the bridge.

Chills ran down Samuel's spine as he too saw what was fast approaching.

"Hard a' starboard!" he ordered his crew, who immediately began taking whatever manoeuvres they could to avoid the incoming rocks.

Olivia gripped onto the railing as the ship narrowly passed the rocks, and as they proceeded along the nearest point of the ship, she sensed a slight relief. A few moments passed of nothing, but the fog remained thick. Resetting her gaze forward she saw to her horror that another large set of rocks was dead ahead after the sharp turn, and she knew there was no way they were avoiding this next set.

"My God," Samuel muttered as he and the crew saw what was ahead of them, and too close for a full evasive move.

"Keep turning to starboard!" he shouted to the crew.

Moments later, Thomas ran out to Olivia to try and bring her inside, but as he reached her, they both knew the impact was imminent. The full scale of the rocks which are almost ship height became apparent as the fog lifted its veil to show the full extent of the area all too late. Thomas and Olivia grabbed onto the railing hard with all of the grips they could muster and then it happened. The rocks collided with the right of the ship and it juddered violently as parts of rock broke off and began littering the front decks of the ship.

The force knocked Olivia and Thomas down to the ground, and they looked up and as the juddering stopped, the large rock passed by and disappeared from sight as quickly as it arrived. The ship came to a halt moments later, and deep down they both knew that it was a very serious incident.

"Stop the ship! We need to assess the damage as quickly as possible!" Samuel could be heard ordering the crew in the bridge.

The late evening storm clouds began to slightly lift and an eerie grey filter seemed to be applied to the environment ahead. Olivia and Thomas stood up and dusted themselves off.

"Are you okay?" asked Thomas.

"Yes, thank you," she replied.

They looked ahead and saw a large island looming in the near distance. A rocky coastline was all they could see, but beyond it seemed to be quite a large landmass.

"Do you think this is what we have been looking for?" Thomas enquired.

"It could be. If it is, it has found us."

They felt the ship come to a halt just past the cluster of rocks.

"Come on, let's go and see what is happening," suggested Thomas.

They re-entered the bridge and saw the crew had dispersed and had gone to other parts of the ship. Samuel was wildly walking around giving orders and taking in the magnitude of the situation.

"What is the situation?" asked Thomas.

"The ship's radio is out, and we are cut off. We won't sink as we are pumping the water out fast enough, but we are going to be here for a little while," Samuel replied.

"Do you have any satellite phones?"

"Yes, but we aren't getting any signal here. We need to be on higher ground for a better chance."

"How high?" Olivia asked.

"I'm not sure. Maybe 25 metres up? It depends as we are in a very remote location."

"As it's still light, maybe we could try and get ashore and look for help? Or at least attempt to get a signal to send a distress call."

"It's too risky as we don't know where we are."

"It could be what we have been looking for though. If that is the case, it's likely to be a deserted ruin. While you repair, maybe it is a good shot to try?" said Thomas.

"And we can see if this island we have been looking for has found us," added Olivia.

"Okay. Take one of the lifeboats to shore, and go with Travis and a few others. He can guide the ship over safely and could help protect you if there is any dangerous wildlife. We need to remember that we don't know what we are walking into."

"Are you sure you don't need the manpower to try and repair the ship?"

"We have a dedicated engineering team already on it, so it is fine."

Samuel turned and headed to a nearby cupboard and got out a satellite phone and some radios.

"Use these, to keep in contact with each other and us on board," he said as he handed Thomas and Olivia a radio set each.

"What channel?"

"The ship radio is setting three, and the channel for the two radios is one."

"Okay, got it," confirmed Thomas.

"Now go and grab whatever you may need, and meet me back here so we can launch you as quickly as possible while we still have some light no matter how grey it may be."

After taking around ten minutes to get changed and grab a small bag with minimal supplies, Olivia met back with everyone else at the bridge.

"Ready?" Travis said, poking his head around the corner of the door.

"Ready," confirmed Olivia, with everyone else nodding in agreement.

"Okay, follow me," replied Travis.

They walked along the deck and to a lifeboat that was ready to be lowered. Two men, David and Andrew, stood by ready to operate it. They both had boots, dark trousers and a jumper on with gloves, which formed a casual uniform. David had short hair while Andrew had a longer style on top with a faded buzz cut.

"Hi, I'm David and this is Andrew," David said, as he introduced himself to everyone.

"We will be coming along with you, to help manoeuvre the boat and because, well, we fancy a little adventure. Your story has captured our imagination, so even if the current circumstance isn't ideal, we couldn't miss coming along," added Andrew.

"That is if you don't mind?" asked David.

"Of course we don't. I don't think we could go without you anyway," confirmed Olivia.

A large thud was heard as Travis dropped a large bag into the boat and stepped on. A butt of a rifle was hanging out confirming; it was a bag of assorted weapons, something that Samuel seemed to highlight earlier as to fend off any unknown wildlife.

"Sorry to interrupt. Are we ready to go?"

"Of course, everyone, get aboard. Let's get this show on the road," said Andrew.

Everyone got on the boat and it was slowly lowered down into the sea. Andrew disconnected the ropes once they reached sea level, and they began to move off, heading towards the coastline which appeared to be within fifty metres. Thomas looked up and saw Olivia looking very thoughtful.

"Are you ready for this?" he asked.

"Yes, I think so," she replied.

"I wonder if this is the place," Travis said.

"It is in the area we were searching, so I think it could be," Thomas added.

"Well, there is only one way to find out," said Callum.

"When we do reach land, everyone, stay close. We don't know what is going to be there to greet us," warned Travis.

After a short journey from the ship, they brought the boat up to the coastline and made landfall. Andrew threw a rope against one of the nearby rocks, and got out and tied it so the lifeboat was secure on the edge of the sea. Everyone got up and left the boat. Taking in the surroundings, they had landed on small stony ground with a large rock face on the right blocking any progress that way, and to the left was a long stretch of coastline that was very narrow and didn't seem to go anywhere. Ahead they could see two rocky hillsides that came together to form a path that led upwards.

"That seems to be the best way forward just up there," Travis advised.

"Agreed," Thomas responded.

"Come on then, follow me," replied Travis.

The group moved forward along the trail in front of them, and they soon reached a section of the rocky hills that had two imposing stone figures, one on each side of the pathway. They were around four to five metres tall, and although eroded away with time, still made out two large godlike beings, both armed and looking out towards the sea.

"Well, that's ominous…" remarked Lauren.

"What do you think they are?" asked Travis, looking towards Olivia.

"If this is the place, they could be some kind of figures or gods the people believed to protect them from the outside world. If the stories are right, then they probably won't take kindly to strangers reaching their shores."

"They are kind of creepy if you ask me," David added.

"Yeah, but if this is Arcanum then the islanders were likely wiped out thousands of years ago, so don't worry too much," said Lauren.

"Come on, we had better not stop to worry about it. We don't have much daylight left, and we need to reach higher ground," Travis said, as he gestured to move further inland.

"You're right, let's go," replied Olivia.

The group headed a few steps forward and saw that just behind each statue was a path, one leading left and one right.

"The path splits in two here," said Thomas.

"Hmm. The left one seems to continue uphill, whereas the right path goes down and seems to lead into those caves just there. It looks pretty dangerous as well with the jagged rocky ground," Travis said, as he surveyed the area.

"With that in mind, I think we should go left. Besides, we are trying to get to higher ground as quickly as possible," added Olivia.

"Okay, let's move," agreed Travis.

They all began heading up the hill and carried on moving between the rocks. After a few minutes of walking, Olivia noticed a small opening in the rocky hillside that caught her attention.

"Hold on," Olivia informed the group.

"What is it?" asked Travis.

"There is an opening here that looks to be substantial inside once you get past the narrow void here. Can I borrow a torch please?"

"Here you go," Thomas said, as he handed over his torch.

"Thanks."

"Be careful in there."

Olivia nodded and cautiously moved into the crack, shimmying her way through. As she reached the inside, she fell forward slightly. She regained her footing and clicked the torch on, shining it around her new surroundings. Around her, she saw that it was a small cave, which was barely a few inches higher than she is. Nothing caught her eye as she moved the torch around.

"Find anything?" Thomas shouted through the crack.

Olivia carried on aiming the torch around as she replied.

"No, there isn't anything... wait a minute."

Her torchlight caught something mysterious against the back of the cave wall. She moved forward slightly and as it came into view, a slight bit of excitement was released within her. She saw a faded but still legible painting on the back wall.

"There is something here, a painting on the wall. Come and have a look."

Within a few moments, Thomas pushed himself through and walked over to Olivia to see what she was looking at.

"That is incredible."

The painting depicted what seemed to be two deities, possibly the two they had just passed, standing over and protecting dozens of human figures who were knelt in front of them. Above the gods were faded outlines of flames, being stopped from hitting the islanders below.

"It appears to show the gods, that are presumably the statues just back there, protecting the islanders from harm. I would make an educated guess that the fire coming from the sea is a representation of any outsiders," said Olivia.

"I think you are right, and that is what we are. Let's hope that as this looks thousands of years old that whoever depicted it is long gone."

"This definitely gives hope to us finding what we are looking for. This sort of depiction would make sense if Arcanum does exist as the islanders would have naturally been fearful of any outsiders, especially after an attack."

"You are right. Come on, let's get back to the group."

They both moved towards the exit and shimmied out through the crack in the rocks.

"What did you see?" enquired Lauren.

"There is a really faint painting on the back of the cave wall of the statues that we passed back there. It seemed to be protecting the island from outside harm," replied Olivia.

"So that means that someone has been here before? I guess that is promising for our search, but it is very eerie," Callum added.

"It makes me uneasy if I'm honest," said Lauren, a little lower than usual.

"I am sure it's nothing to worry about. Besides, if the bogeyman does decide to appear, I have this," Travis said as he smiled and hoisted his rifle up a little in his arms, in an attempt to reassure Lauren.

"Let's keep moving," Olivia said, as she touched Lauren on the shoulder.

A short distance further up the track the ground levelled out, and they came to a few trees. Moving through, they entered a larger, more open area.

"Oh, wow," Olivia said, a little taken aback.

In front of the group was a series of collapsed stone ruins, which seemed to have been small dwellings for settlers.

"Are these…some kind of ruins from homes?" asked Callum.

"Quite possibly," Thomas responded, as he and Olivia headed over to one to take a closer look. The roof of the one they looked inside had long gone, and other than a few smashed items including what appeared to be an empty case, plate and rotting wooden table, there wasn't much there. It was clear although this had been a ruin for thousands of years, it was what someone had once called home.

"It doesn't look like anyone has been in here for hundreds if not thousands of years. This one doesn't even have a roof," Olivia said as she looked around.

"These clues are definitely hinting that some kind of settlement was here in the past. No evidence it is what we are looking for yet, but it is promising," Thomas added.

"I think the painting we saw seems to be the strongest matching clue so far, but let's carry on moving and see what else we find," said Olivia.

"Look, there is a gap in the trees ahead. Maybe that leads to higher ground,' Travis said, pointing to an area just north of where they are."

Everyone nodded in agreement, and they passed the last crumbled ruin and entered the old beaten path through the undergrowth that led into an area surrounded by trees. Within ten or so metres, the trees around them suddenly became very dense and the little evening light that remained suddenly dimmed greatly.

"It will be harder to track time if the light in here is this restricted. We need to move through this area as quickly as possible, and try to stick to the path. We can't afford to get lost in here," Travis advised.

The soundscape directly contrasted with the one outside of the trees, as a near deathly silence only disturbed by their footsteps and movement was present. The change in atmosphere was recognised by everyone, as the whole group became silent and focused more on hand gestures to advance forward.

All of a sudden a movement through the trees was heard which wasn't coming from the group. Hard to hear at first, a rustling through the trees and the accompanying twig snapping began to get louder, alerting the group. Travis held his hand up silently, gesturing for everyone to stop immediately. They did and slowly formed a tighter formation together as they stood lower to the ground.

The noise began to intensify and circle around them fast. Something, or someone, appeared to be hunting them. The rushing noise got really close as if something was about to make its presence visible, but then it suddenly, and rather unexpectedly, stopped.

Chapter Thirteen

An eerie silence gripped the trees and made Olivia feel extremely vulnerable. Travis took a few steps forward and scanned the environment as much as possible in the dim light. Looking left to right his eyes began to adjust, and he was unable to see anything that could have dashed around them.

Assuming it was just a small animal that wasn't a threat he lowered his gun and turned to face Olivia. He was met with an expression of pure horror. Olivia stood rooted to the spot staring just behind Travis. He turned slowly round and saw it. A dark figure, humanoid in build, stood evenly in between two trees around ten metres ahead directly in front of them. The figure was in the shadows, motionless and without expression.

"He... hello?" Travis spluttered, quieter and lacking his usual confidence.

Travis moved slowly towards the figure, gun half up and unsure if what he was looking at was a threat. The figure didn't move and stood its ground as Travis got closer.

"Our erm... ship... Our ship has run aground down on the coast, and we are just trying to find some help. We don't mean any..."

Travis stopped speaking suddenly and went silent. He looked down and turned to face the group. Olivia put her hand to her mouth in horror as she saw an arrow had hit Travis directly in the chest and had come through, pointing out towards her. He stumbled a few steps towards the group before collapsing and dying. Olivia felt the world slow as her senses heightened through a cocktail of fear and adrenaline.

"HIDE!" Thomas shouted to everyone, and Olivia and Lauren darted into a nearby bush and got as low as possible.

Callum, Thomas, David and Andrew rushed forward to the now lifeless body of Travis. As Thomas realised he was dead, an islander ran from behind the figure and kicked him down to the ground. He was armed with a sharp knife and went to slash Thomas in the throat. Andrew shot the islander as he was mere inches from making contact with the blade.

Thomas looked up and nodded a thank you, but at that very moment, a large blade cut into Andrew, and he was knocked to the ground by the killer and one other attacker. Thomas got to his feet, but he and Callum were immediately grabbed by the islanders, now numbering five and were dragged along the ground and towards where the dark figure was. David opened fire but after barely letting off a few bullets his gunfire ceased as he was hit with two quick consecutive arrows, one in the arm and one in the leg, knocking him down immediately.

Only barely able to see what was going on through the bushes, Olivia was unsure of what was happening. Lauren looked at her, scared. She peered out and was immediately grabbed by another islander. Lauren began to scream loudly as she was thrown over the shoulder of a large male islander, who immediately began taking her away.

Olivia ran out of the bushes after her and was confronted with a terrifying scene. She saw Travis and Andrew sprawled on the floor dead with blood coating the soil. Everyone else was being forcibly carried away by five islanders whose faces were hidden by the shadows of the trees. As Olivia was met with the horror in front of her, she was briefly frozen to the spot with indecision. She didn't know what to do as everyone had been overpowered by the attackers in a flurry of panic and confusion.

"RUN OLIVIA! GET BACK TO THE SHIP AND WARN THE OTHERS!" Thomas shouted.

"But…" she protested, wanting to help but not knowing what to do.

"GO!" Thomas shouted again, and with that, she saw herself becoming surrounded from all angles except the rear by numerous islanders, emerging from the trees. She decided to take the advice, turned and ran, against her inner desire to stay and find some way to stop the attackers.

Picking up into a near-immediate sprint, Olivia made her way back along the route the group came. The islanders were hot on her tail, and it wasn't long until shouts from the attackers were heard all around. As she reached the path, they used to enter the trees, an islander blocked her way and drew a bow and arrow. Feeling sick with horror at the sight of this, she used her adrenaline to power on, and moved to the right and deeper into the trees.

More arrows flew near her body as she darted through the ever darker area, not truly knowing where she was going. Making a small lead over the attackers, she saw a large fallen tree and crouched by it, in a hope the attackers would run past so she could double back and try and save everyone. She put her hand over her mouth as the attackers stopped near the tree, shouting at each other in a language she had never heard before. She looked up slightly and one of the islanders saw her and pointed, shouting to his fellow attackers.

Olivia got back up and ran again in the only direction she could, forwards and away from the pursuers. More arrows hit tree branches and flew through the leaves near her as the ground began to take a strong decline. As it got steeper and as exhaustion began to kick in, she tripped and fell forwards on a sudden sharp downhill slope. Momentum and gravity pulled her faster down, and she fell off a small two or so metre high drop, making a thud as she got the wind knocked out of her upon landing.

Still falling, she looked up and saw the numerous figures of the attackers stopped at the top of the fall she had just taken, bows drawn and firing a few more arrows. Olivia soon felt the ground vanish from beneath her and fell down a dark hole, falling a short distance greater than the last. She landed hard and was knocked out on impact, as her body came to a halt in the centre of the darkness.

As she slowly opened her eyes, Olivia sat up confused and slightly dazed. She was in almost complete darkness, so reached for her pocket and her lighter. She flicked it a few times and the spark ignited. The flame revealed she had fallen down an opening that led into the cave she was in.

Seeing nothing but a bare rock in front of her, she stood and turned. Immediately she was confronted with a skeleton hanging upside down, and the skull was level with her head. She recoiled back in horror and at the fearful jolt, it gave her. A wave of shock and horror returned to her body as she looked past the hanging skeleton and saw at the back of the cave a few metres away, there were two more skeletons, these ones propped against the wall.

She walked over and saw that they were both wearing faded uniforms that seem to be that of another ship. Seeing that these individuals were probably attacked like she was before falling down here, she couldn't help but feel an immediate relatable sympathy. It also crossed her mind that she wasn't one of the first people to set foot on the island.

After her mind briefly wandered, Olivia came back to focus on the real crisis at hand. She needed to get back to the ship and warn the others of what just happened and of the real danger of the island. She headed away from the bodies, and in the corner of her eye, she saw an opening in the rocks. She shimmied her way out and stumbled out into an area of jagged rocks.

It was now dark outside, and Olivia realised she must have been knocked out for a few hours at the least which concerned her as that amount of time for her friends would be vital. She advanced the only way she could and soon recognised the area as where the split of the path was just past the statues from earlier on. Climbing up and out of the lower rocky area, she reached the split in the path and began running back down towards the small boat they came to land on. She pushed the boat off the coastline and as it floated into the water she climbed on and began navigating back towards the ship.

Although it was dark, the moonlight gave the area enough visibility and the shadows cast by the ship in the near distance revealed its location. Soon she came up close and saw that the ship was sinking and had a slight angle. The sea was almost level with the front lower deck of the ship, and this worried Olivia as she was under the impression the ship was having the water pumped out, and clearly this had stopped. As she came up beside the ship, she moved around it looking for a way aboard.

Soon she eyed an open portside door, which was close to sea level. Moving the small boat over to the opening, she noticed a bloody handprint on the inside of the portside door. The mere sight brought a strong level of anxiety about entering, as the feeling something bad had happened hit Olivia hard. She tied the rope of the small boat against a small grip by the door and carefully climbed onto the ship.

Olivia entered the corridor and looked to the left which was towards the front of the ship and saw the hallway flooding with water. The only way was right and up the stairs so she moved in that direction. She began to climb the stairs cautiously and as she did she really began to feel the increasing angle the ship was sinking at, as she had to hold the rail and almost hug the wall on one side.

At the top of the stairs, she had reached the hallway that led to the sleeping quarters. There were a few dim lights near to her, and a few rooms had light coming through the open doors. However, the end of the hallway was in complete darkness. She soon passed the room she was in and looked in through the open door.

The room has been ransacked and it was a complete mess. Broken glass knocked over furniture and clothes thrown all over the floor shocked Olivia. She walked a few steps in to look and noticed a photo of Arthur smashed in its frame, looking up at her from the floor. As she laid eyes on it, a loud moaning of steel was briefly heard as the ship carried on its slow descent into the sea.

She left the room immediately upon hearing this and carried on advancing through the hallway. She noticed that the doors to a few more rooms were wide open as well. Something or someone had searched the area high and low, but she didn't know what for and the absence of any crew worried her. Reaching the end of the hall she turned to the left. The door to the canteen was closed and through the glass was only darkness.

Against her own better judgement, she peered through the glass, moving her face up to the glass in a futile attempt at seeing better. Unable to see anything, she slowly opened the door and pulled the door open. A dead body, which was resting against the side of the door away from the window, fell onto Olivia and knocked her down.

As the dead face met hers she saw that the body was that of Chef Sebastian. She threw the body off her in terror and briefly panicked. Now, on the floor, she looked to her right and could see through an open crew door. Another dead crew member was slumped against a wall by their bed, with a frozen expression of anguish.

Blood was all over the floor and a struggle looked to have occurred. Olivia began to have horrible assumptions of what had happened, with the same islanders coming aboard and killing everyone in a way she witnessed on the island coming to mind. Was it mindless violence or did they feel they were being invaded somehow?

She got up and headed through the canteen door. Moving through the canteen, she saw the place has been messed up just like the cabins, with food and cutlery thrown all around. Another dead body was slumped over the serving area table, with a large knife stuck in its back. Recoiling in horror, Olivia headed up a short set of stairs and onto the bridge.

As she entered the bridge, she saw that the floor had a long blood trail that led to the main navigational desk. Over this was the slumped body of Samuel Jones. She looked at him and saw he was expressionless. She turned and something grabbed her arm hard. She screamed and turned to see that Samuel was still barely alive.

"Olivia…" Samuel spluttered, as he attempted to stand.

Due to his wounds, this was futile, and he fell to the ground and sat against the back of the navigational system.

"Samuel! What happened?" Olivia responded, in complete shock.

"A few hours after you left, these savages smashed their way on board and attacked. They killed everyone and disabled the pumps, meaning the ship will sink," he replied.

"We need to get you some first aid; that wound in your side needs treatment at once."

"Why….why are you back here? Where is everyone else?" he asked, having missed what Olivia said.

"Not far onto the island, we were attacked by what seems to be another group of islanders. They killed Travis, David and Andrew and have taken everyone else away. I managed to get away and Thomas ordered me to get back and warn everyone here, but it looks like I was too late. I was knocked out for a few hours on my way back here and I fear that was when you were attacked. I'm so sorry for bringing you here."

"Don't apologise Olivia. You, like your father, are a remarkable human being, but we came here out of our own choice. We chose adventure once more and this one seems to have gotten the better of us."

"You are not going to die, where is the first aid?"

"Over there by the cupboard," he advised, pointing behind Olivia.

She stood and rushed over to it, and returned in a matter of moments. Opening it up, she got out some bandages and immediately began applying them to the open wound on Samuel's side.

"This will help stop the bleeding."

"Okay. Can you pass me my cigar?"

"Erm sure, where is it?"

"Just above me by the main controls."

Olivia grabbed it and Samuel lit it up. He took a long drag and exhaled the smoke away from her. A brief moment of satisfaction crossed his face. He looked up at Olivia and smiled.

"I knew your father well you know. This ship is the one that took him on some of his quests around the world."

"I didn't know it was this exact ship!"

"Yeah, this old girl has been with me for twenty years now. Oh, the fun times we have had together. I was there for a lot of the great moments in your father's career if you could call it that of course."

"I know what you mean as some of it was a little controversial."

"Listen. I know from your fathers passing how hard that losing someone can be. Please, try and save whoever is still alive."

"But it's just me. What can one person do against all of them?"

"You are a 'King' Olivia. Your father was one of the strongest willed people that I have ever known and it is within you as well, you just need to realise your potential. You will find a way to overcome it, just like he would. You might need some firepower, feel free to take anything you may need from downstairs."

As he spoke, Samuel was visibly getting weaker. He took another long smoke on his cigar and looked at Olivia.

"Save as many as you can. Promise me that."

"I promise."

He slightly nodded and removed the cigar from his mouth. He looked down slightly and then fell silent. The cigar dropped from his hand and Olivia knew he had passed away. She briefly felt lost and a little out of the body, but then another grumble of the steel being sucked into the sea was heard. She knew she didn't have much time, so grabbed the radio from her pocket and tried calling Thomas, in the hope he was still alive.

"Thomas, can you hear me? Can anyone hear me? Hello?"

Nothing but static came back on the radio so she tried again.

"Everyone on the ship is dead. I was too late. I need to know if you are still alive."

A few more moments of static were the only form of reply she got.

"I'm coming back to look for you. If you can hear me, please radio back to me as soon as you can."

She turned the radio off and put it back in her pocket.

"Damn it!" she frustratingly muttered to herself.

Another groan from the ship was heard through the room and it juddered for a few moments quite aggressively. She rushed to the front window of the bridge and saw the front of the boat was going under water fast. She needed to get off the ship as soon as possible, so got up and instinctively darted for the door, only to pause.

Realising she needs weapons, she went back down the stairs she came up and then down the second flight of stairs and along the hall that led to the lower crew quarters and armoury. She saw that the door to the armoury was half open with a body slumped beside it, giving the assumption a futile move to get weapons was made before. At the end of the hall, water could be seen and was advancing on Olivia fast. Knowing she had a very small window of opportunity she entered the armoury, which was a small storeroom of assorted weapons.

Travis and the others had taken the majority with them when heading to the island earlier, but a small chest remained in the corner of the room unopened. Inside she found two handguns and ammo. She picked these up as well as the belt with holsters and room for ammo and put it around her waist. The sound of water rushing up the hall increased and within moments it was at her feet and gaining depth fast.

She looked out of the room and saw the end of the hall was already nearly fully underwater, such was the angle the ship was now taking. She moved back into the room and grabbed a knife that was on the shelf and added it to her belt. She turned to leave and the water was now waist height. Another rumble echoed through the hall and then the few lights in the hall dimmed and went off.

She climbed back up the stairs and all the way up to the bridge. She ran out onto the deck and saw the water was up to the bridge externally and the ship probably had a matter of minutes left above the sea. Making her way to the middle of the deck, she saw that she was too far out to swim to the island. She grabbed a lifejacket from the deck and put it on immediately. She ran over to the side of the ship that she tied her boat too and looked down.

The door she'd tied the boat to was now too far under water and had vanished from view, but due to the length of rope from the boat, remarkably it hadn't been pulled under with the ship yet. As the sinking of the ship picked up the pace and she could see the bridge begin to disappear under the waves, she made a quick decision and jumped off the ship, landing near the boat. She quickly pulled herself on board and grabbed her knife. She began cutting at the rope which was starting to pull the boat down.

She managed to cut the rope and as the link to the sinking ship was tethered, the boat lurched back as the tension was released. She immediately began to move away from the ship as quickly as possible, and within a few moments, she watched as the last of the ship was swallowed into the shallow sea bed. As the sea, where the ship was moments ago, returned to a flat surface like nothing had happened, Olivia became briefly overcome with emotion. A tear ran down her face as she realised just how severe and ever direr the situation was becoming. With what Samuel had said moments ago racing through her mind, she regained some focus and took the boat to the nearest part of the island she could.

Olivia pulled the boat out of the water and without a rope to tie it anymore, positioned it nestled in between two small trees in the hope it wouldn't be taken away when the tide came in any further. She checked she had everything and headed into the treeline, but as she didn't recognise this part of the island, her only hope was to proceed forward in search of any clues that could lead to her missing friends.

Chapter Fourteen

Olivia began to move through the wooded area with a quicker pace about her. She knew that time was really running out, especially as she had been unconscious for a fair few hours. She ran along a fairly beaten track surrounded by trees and lush greenery. Alongside her was a river that was flowing fast downstream, and in the direction she was heading, and as she stopped for a brief moment of rest, the sound of the water rushing past briefly soothed her.

Closing her eyes Olivia took a few deep breaths and then felt a small vibration in her pocket. She instinctively moved her hand to the source and pulled out the satellite phone. It had vibrated to indicate that signal was now available, although only a weak one. She immediately dialled the emergency number drilled into her by Thomas and Samuel and hit call. The number seemed to connect although there was only a very faint static sound.

"Mayday! Mayday! This is Olivia King of the Adventurer. We are stranded on an island in the South Pacific Ocean and need immediate rescue. Please respond!"

She paused for a moment before repeating.

"Mayday! Mayday! I say again, this is Olivia King of the Adventurer. We are stranded on an island in the South Pacific Ocean and need immediate rescue. Please respond!"

A rustling in the trees behind her was heard faintly, but she was too distracted by the excitement of having a lifeline potentially granted.

"We have been attacked by islanders, and some of the crew have been murdered. Our ship has sunk, and we are completely stranded. Please, can anyone hear me?"

A brief moment of silence followed before a male voice came through the phone.

"SART Base to Olivia, we read you. Say again? Please state your location and the nature of your emergency."

"Thank God, I…" Olivia began, but she was struck from behind and knocked to the ground mid-sentence.

She dropped the phone in shock and it fell into the river. Olivia's eyes followed it as it vanished from view. She turned and could see two bulky male islanders had hit her and were preparing to do so again. Both were in simple dirty cloth attire with long scraggly hair.

One of the men strode forward and picked Olivia up and struck her in the face with a bare hand before throwing her to the ground by a large rock. The attacker shouted at the other present, pointing at Olivia with pure aggression. The second male then drew a bow and arrow and pulled it back ready to fire. He headed close to Olivia and had the arrow aimed close to her face.

"Please, stop!" Olivia pleaded in a panic as she started to slowly move back on her hands and rear.

The men, who showed no remorse or understanding, shouted louder with the other man who hit her moments ago holding up an axe. The man yelled and began running towards her to strike when gunshots rang out. In a knee jerk survivalist reaction, Olivia drew her handgun and fired at both men, taking them out in a flurry of shots. She didn't stop firing until the gun emptied, and even then she pulled the trigger a few more times.

Both men crumbled to the floor almost as quickly as the gunshots erupted, and Olivia looked forward in shock. Adrenaline was pumping hard, and she heard her heart pounding in her head. She dropped the gun to the ground and moved herself up against the back of the rock. She was covered in blood on her upper body and seemed to be taken away from the moment as it is so surreal. She had just killed two people.

She stood after a moment and headed straight to the river, and saw the phone was completely gone. Looking down and into the water, she saw her reflection and immediately put her hands into the river and started washing the blood and dirt off her face. After this, she started following the river again for a short distance and discovered that the river came to a short waterfall. In any eventuality, the satellite phone was gone.

This briefly crushed Olivia, as she couldn't see any other way of communicating with the world away from the island. She just hoped deep down that the very brief moment she spoke with someone was heard and was enough. She headed back to where she was attacked and picked up her handgun and reloaded. Glancing down at one of the crumbled bodies, she noticed the bow and arrow. She picked it up and stretched the bow back a few times, and realised it felt like one of the cheaper models she used as a child and decided it may have some use.

Taking the small number of arrows from the body, she put the bow over her back and the arrows in her belt. Turning with her back towards the waterfall, Olivia entered an opening in the rock face and moved forward. Not far in she could see light coming in from above her, and a ledge around five metres up. She knew she couldn't jump up that high but could see alongside it some rocks sticking out that she could use to climb up. She checked her hands were not slippery and began to climb up.

At the highest point she could climb, she looked and saw she was still a little off level with the ledge, so she jumped, and caught the edge of the surface with just her hands, as her body hit the edge of the rocks. She pulled herself up and kept moving.

The rocky surroundings turned into a larger open area, and she entered what looked to be a tomb. As she slowly walked forward in awe, she saw a sacrificial area. In front of her was a skeleton, hanging in the air above a hole in the ground.

The skeleton had its arms stretched out wide and tied crudely against the tomb walls. There were remnants of an altar beside it, which was adorned with a few sharp blades and a few assorted artefacts. A faded symbol was chalked on the rear wall of the tomb, and it appeared to match that of the artefact. Olivia wondered if this was a sign of a religious or cult symbol.

She moved towards the hole and looked down. It was too dark so she shone her torch and saw that it was some sort of burial pit with various bones from skeletons, some complete and some just parts, littering the pit floor. It became obvious that at some point in time, this room was routinely used to kill people and to throw the remains into this pit.

Turning away, she noticed a body slumped against the wall beside her. This one caught her eye as it was clothed in the same uniform as the bodies she saw in the cavern she'd fallen into earlier when escaping the islanders. Curious, she moved over to take a look.

In the top pocket of the uniform, she noticed a small collection of papers that appeared to be in the form of a small logbook. She pulled them out carefully and saw that they were still legible. This may be a chance to understand what happened to this individual, the other scattered crew she has seen, and potentially provide an insight as to what happened. She cast her eyes on the first page and began reading.

Stephen was right, there was something out here in this vast ocean. He said there was an ancient island, and that it held a mystery that humanity needed to discover. I agree with the former, there is an island here. But it is something that needs to be left hidden.

If there is ever proof of hell on earth existing, I have seen it with my own eyes. After smashing into this godforsaken place, I knew it was not going to bode well. I and a few others headed inland in hope of finding help, but what we uncovered was the farthest from help. The huts by the river that we came across did not house warmth or assistance, they housed the souls of the devil himself.

We were attacked by dozens of natives, and many of us were killed right there. I managed to escape into the woods with a few others and kept them on our trail initially, to make sure they did not head from where we came and discover our ship. But then when it came to losing them, it was very difficult. We soon made it to higher ground and, after dealing with some of the just as friendly wildlife here, we made it to a temple.

For a place as savage as this, it was beautiful, and I saw some of the most treasured artefacts of this Earth. But there was no time for looting, we needed to get back to the ship and warn the others. Help was not here, we could only help ourselves. They need to know this.

Olivia turned the page and found another entry, this one in more rushed handwriting than the previous.

They found us, we thought we had lost them, but they were on us the entire time. Once we cleared the temple area and were heading through another large structure that seemed to lead into a wooded area, we were ambushed. The only survivors, if you could call us that, were Stephen and myself. We were dragged to this small tomb and have been left here for hours. We need to get out, but I can't find a way. I will, I must.

Olivia turned the page and there was one last entry. She started to read, feeling as if she was aware of the way the story ends.

I have failed him. Those bastards hung Stephen up right in front of me and stuck a blade deep into his heart, draining his soul in front of me and leaving him to hang over the pit below. They beat me and then left, keeping one of my hands tied to the wall. It is dim, but I can still see by the flickering candlelight Stephen just hanging there. I cannot bear it. Even when I close my eyes, he is there. I cannot do this anymore, I just cannot. Forgive me.

The entry stopped suddenly and Olivia couldn't help but feel sorry for the person who wrote it. She looked upon the skull with its locked open jaw and began to imagine the look of terror that would have been across the face the moment he died. She placed the diary back in the pocket and turned and looked upon the hanging skeleton with a little more context. The remnants of whatever civilisation that once prospered here are now savages, and sacrificial rituals seemed to be a common activity.

This gave way to a deeper fear of the same fate being met by everyone who has been taken captive from her group, and she knew time was running out.

Looking for a way out of the tomb, she paced around before finding a very thin and crumbled looking section of wall, which Olivia could see light coming through the cracks. Knowing she could probably knock it down and proceed, she looked around and saw a long object similar to a crowbar on the ground. Olivia picked it up and took a few swings at the wall, which crumbled more with each hit.

After three or four impacts, a hole was made to which she put the object in and pried it back towards her, which made an opening just wide enough for her to slip through. She threw the object down and slipped out and saw that she was on a grassy area, which had a high vantage point over the island. Although dark, the moonlight danced around the trees that faded off into the distance and painted a beautiful outline.

For a brief moment, she fixated on it and wished she was somewhere else as peaceful as the view suggested. She pulled out the radio and decided to try Thomas again.

"Thomas, are you there? Please respond!" Olivia pleaded into the radio but was met by the same radio silence as before.

"If you are alive, please respond."

After a few moments, a voice responded.

"Olivia?" Thomas faintly replied.

"Thomas? It is so good to hear you. Are you okay? Where are you?"

"I… I don't know. I've been unconscious. I was taken away by these monsters and now I am in a guarded area of woods."

"I managed to get back to the ship. Everyone had been killed, it was a bloodbath."

"Oh, God…"

"And the ship has sunk. It was sinking when I got there, and it went under shortly after. Are you with Lauren, Callum and David?"

"Lauren, Callum and David are here. David has been really hurt, but Lauren and Callum aren't badly injured. We are all just shaken. Where are you now?"

"I'm headed back inland, looking for you. I'm on a high vantage point at the moment, looking over a hilltop."

"Hmm, it's quite likely if we make some kind of signal you might see us. Hang on…"

A moment of silence that goes on longer for what Olivia would like occurs before Thomas comes back on.

"I still have a flare in my possession. If I fire this up, they are sure to catch us, but you are our only chance of getting away from them."

"Okay, do it."

A moment passed and then suddenly in the distance, a flare went up, lighting up the skyline to the north. Shouting from multiple voices then cut through on the radio.

"Shit!" Thomas was heard saying before the radio immediately went dead.

The very second this happened, Olivia not taking her eye off the dying light of the flare, remembered the location and began to run towards it with all the energy she could muster. It wasn't far, and she could be there in a minute or so if her judgement of the distance was correct.

She ran down an embankment, and through the trees towards the source of the flare. She soon got close and climbed down a small rocky face landing behind some bushes. Through these, she saw a large group of islanders, all loudly chanting and looking forward. Over them, she saw Thomas, Lauren, David and Callum, tied up against a few pillars. They were in the pose she saw in the tomb that displayed the ritual sacrifices, and she realised this is what the islanders have planned. She had little time.

Olivia moved slowly forward. She looked through the bush and saw a masked man stood in front of the crew, waving a sharp weapon. Drums started beating from the crowd, and a ritual seemingly began.

As the drumming slowly intensified, the crowd started to yell and scream in a choral manner. She saw the masked man approach David and slit him with the blade in his abdomen and throat, with blood pouring over the floor and onto the ritual stones. The crowd cheered and the man turned to bait the crowd into an increased frenzy. He then turned and pointed his weapon at Lauren.

With instinct, Olivia lit the end of her arrows and fired two at different parts of the area, causing a fire to spread. This caused panic and the crowd began to scatter. Using this as cover, she dropped the bow and arrow and moved sneakily around and got behind the crew. She moved forward and began to untie Thomas.

As she started, the masked man turned and saw what was going on. He moved to attack and Olivia shot him with the handgun. This alerted some of the nearby islanders who came back over to attack. Thomas was freed and given the handgun.

Olivia cut free the others while Thomas held off the islanders with the handgun. Once they were all free, Thomas fired a few more bullets towards the islanders giving them enough room to retreat into the forest behind.

After running for a few minutes and gaining some distance from the islanders, everyone came to a halt outside of a darkened cave entrance.

"Let's find some cover in here!" Thomas panted, pointing into the cave.

Entering the cave, everyone shuffled towards the furthest corner away from the view of anyone that may look in from the way they just came. Thomas looked around and quickly found some wood for a makeshift fire. They were far enough around the corner in his mind to get away with some faint light, but his concern for how cold it was outweighed any concern of being spotted.

He knelt down and struck his lighter a few times before it took hold and the spark ignited a small fire that quickly warmed the cave. He sat back against the rocky wall of the cave and looked over towards the rest of the group. They were all speechless, with a mix of horror and anxiety across their faces. He smiled faintly at Olivia.

"Thank you for coming back for us," he said.

"Yeah, you saved us, and just in time. Thank you," added Lauren.

"It's okay, really," Olivia responded.

"Do you think we have really found what we were looking for?" enquired Callum.

"It seems to have found us. This place, it's horrific. Far from being decimated, they seem to have been surviving all this time," said Olivia.

"What happened to you Olivia while you were gone?" Thomas asked, coming closer and placing his hand on her face, looking over the mix of dirt, a little blood and a mark on her side.

"When you told me to run, I didn't want to. I wanted to stay and fight, but I knew you were right. I had to get back to the ship and warn everyone. I ran as fast as I could and a lot of those savages came after me, firing arrows and trying to kill me."

"Did they hurt you in any way?" queried Lauren.

"No, I managed to get away, but only because I slipped and fell down a slope and into a hole in the ground. It must have only been a four or five-metre drop, but it knocked me unconscious for a while. When I regained consciousness, I headed straight for the ship. It was a nightmare. I guess you didn't tell them?"

"No. When I got off the radio to you, I was caught by the bastards who were preparing to kill us," Thomas replied.

"Tell us what?" Callum asked, leaning forward.

"When I got to the ship and moved my way through the decks it became clear that the islanders had found the ship and had attacked. Everyone was dead and the place was trashed."

Everyone except Thomas who had already had time to let this all process reacted with shock and gasps.

"I reached the bridge and found Samuel. He was still alive, and he told me about what happened, and he died in my arms."

Olivia looked over to Thomas and touched his arm, knowing talking about it would have an effect as it was one of his closest friends.

"I'm so sorry Thomas," Olivia said, trying to comfort him.

"It's okay," he replied quietly before looking up at Olivia with a teary eye. "Keep going, what happened after?"

"The ship began to sink so I ran down to the armoury that was mentioned prior and grabbed the very few pieces of guns and gear I have with me now. As I was in the armoury, water began pouring into the ship, and I managed to get to the upper deck and get off with the lifeboat we came ashore on the first time just as the ship sank below the water. I headed inland and made contact with SART. But as I was talking, I was attacked by a few islanders. I managed to stop them but the phone, it…"

"The satellite phone, do you still have it Olivia?" asked Thomas.

"No."

Lauren's face seemed to lose the final thread of hope she had upon hearing this.

"How are we going to get out of here? What are we even to do next? We are lost on an island in the middle of nowhere with a bunch of murderous islanders bearing down on us!" Lauren said with an outburst of panic.

"I, I don't know…"

"Did they get enough information from you?" Callum wondered.

"I told them who we were, and where we are, then I was attacked. I don't know if the message was understood as the signal wasn't great. But I am sure they heard at least the name of our ship and the ocean we are in."

"They must have heard. They must have heard?" Lauren said, extremely anxious.

"I am sure they did. After that, I headed through a cave and found a tomb, which had a skeleton inside hanging with its arms stretched and tied, and below it was a pit full of bones. That is how I knew you guys were in serious trouble as they seem to sacrifice anyone who is an outsider."

"So you don't think we are the first here?" asked Callum.

"No, not at all. In this tomb, I found skeletal remains that were in faded clothing, that of another ship. In the pocket of the shirt were a few scraps from a log, and I read it. It appears another ship in near-identical circumstances came across this island, and the crew came inland for help but were decimated."

"So they all died?"

"I don't know, but the diary seemed to suggest they were in serious trouble."

"Serious trouble? That is an understatement. And here we are, like them, totally screwed!" said Lauren, in a slightly raised and panicked voice.

"Calm down. What we need to do is try and catch some rest and then figure out what we are going to do. We are being seemingly hunted and in surroundings of which we do not know. If we are to survive we need to be thinking rationally," Thomas added.

"I agree. We are deep in a cavern, and the light from the fire shouldn't be giving us away. Let's get some rest," recommended Olivia, who stood and placed her hand reassuringly on Lauren's shoulder before walking back and further into the cave. Everyone nodded in agreement and began to settle in. Nothing else was said, and within half an hour, everyone fell asleep.

Chapter Fifteen

Olivia stirred and opened her eyes a short time later. Looking around her she saw everyone was fast asleep, and this made her feel a small sense of relief, as she knew that the horrible events so far had drained the team, and she feared there would be more testing times to come. She stared into the darkness in the corner of the cave, beyond the fading light of the fire and saw a shadow dart across the wall, back and forth. The thought that maybc this was what caused her to wake crossed her mind, and she could see whatever it was definitely wasn't human.

Olivia kept her focus on the corner of the cave and what appeared to be the source of the shadows. Her eyes began to focus and make out what was lurking in the darkness. Then a sense of dread flooded her bones, as a set of piercing eyes slowly appeared from the corner, and a wolf crept forward into the light. Olivia slowly sat up and without time to react the wolf attacked.

It jumped on top of Olivia, trying to bite repeatedly at her upper body and neck. Trying with all she could to hold the wolf away it quickly became apparent that she was no match for its sheer strength. The wolf got the upper hand and lunged for her throat when suddenly the wolf lost all of its frenzies.

Thomas had rushed over and slashed the wolf with his hunting knife and repeatedly cut into it. The wolf fell off Olivia and collapsed to the floor. During the commotion, everyone else had woken up.

"Are you okay Olivia?" Thomas asked, looking her directly in the eyes.

"Yes, thank you."

"It's clear now that the islanders didn't follow us in here because this is a wolf den. We need to leave, now!" stated Thomas, who began frantically picking up his things.

Everyone else followed suit immediately, and they all hastily left the cave. As they went outside, they could see it was now early morning. It was still dim, but the sun was beginning to rise. They all headed along the path ahead, which led them up a slight gradient. The trees became dense, hiding the dawn glow and keeping the darkness within. Only breaks of light through the odd gap in the trees lit the way. Thomas had taken the lead and was up ahead with Callum, leaving Olivia and Lauren half a dozen metres behind.

"Are you doing okay? You had me worried back there Lauren," asked Olivia.

"Yeah, I am okay, sorry. I didn't mean to snap at you like that, it's just that this has been, and still is, hard for me."

"No, it's fine. This is tough on all of us. I didn't know that this was the reality of the place and that we would be placed in such danger. It is me who should apologise, for bringing you to this place."

"You promised an adventure, and we are getting it. Not quite the one advertised, I must say but an adventure nonetheless," Lauren replied, with half a smile breaking across her face.

"I guess you are right there, I guess you are right."

"Hey, you two; you have got to see this," Callum called down towards them.

Olivia and Lauren picked up the pace and headed over to Callum and Thomas who had both stopped and were staring ahead. Olivia and Lauren took a few more steps, and they were met with a stunning view of a valley below, which was slowly being lit up by the morning sun.

"It's…breath taking," Olivia said quietly.

"I didn't know such a place of savagery could look so beautiful," stated Thomas.

"Look down there, there is a temple or something to the left of the valley," Lauren remarked, pointing just out of Olivia's field of view.

"We should take a look. It may have some clues as to where we really are," Thomas added.

"Yeah, okay, if we head down the hill we should be able to reach it via that route there," agreed Olivia, pointing along the side of the hill.

They followed the trail down and came to the bottom in a few minutes. Everyone looked up and could see a large stone building that appeared to be some sort of place of worship. A few statues that were similar to what they passed earlier adorned the two highest corners of the building and the two sides of the doorway that led the way inside.

"Okay, let's head inside," Olivia said as she took the lead and walked in.

They entered the temple and slowly began to break away from each other, looking around the main hall they found themselves in. Olivia walked towards a wall full of detailed illustrations. The first few that she saw were of depictions of ships full of demons landing on a beach.

The next was a series that showed the demons attacking innocents and destroying the island. Olivia quickly realised that the illustrations showed the attack that destroyed Arcanum thousands of years ago. A flush of emotion hit her as she realised she had without a doubt discovered the island.

"Hey, take a look at these," Olivia called over to everyone, who headed over immediately.

"What is it?" Thomas asked.

"These illustrations show the attack from the northern continent that destroyed this place thousands of years ago. Before this moment, this island was a thriving civilisation, but they came and devastated it."

"Incredible," Thomas added.

Olivia moved towards the centre of the room and took a moment to take it in. She looked forward and saw a few bullet holes in one of the pillars and wall that was directly behind it. A chill ran down her spine as she remembered what was written in the diary she had read earlier.

"What's wrong?" Callum queried, with a concerned look on his face.

"That diary I read in the tomb where the skeleton was hung up…"

"Yeah, I recall you mentioned it. What has it got to do with here?" asked Callum.

"The person writing it said that he and some of the crew he came onto the island with came across this place, and it was an ambush. A lot of them died, presumably, right on this very ground we stand."

"So those bullet holes are from them?" Callum asked, heading over to them to have a closer look.

"I, I think so yes."

Callum placed his fingers along and inside the bullet holes, tracing the surface gently.

"That is eerie. We should be careful, learn from what happened to them."

"Look, up there," remarked Thomas as he held his hand up towards what was drawing his attention.

The illustrations stopped, and the wall led to a set of steps that rose into another chamber.

"It seems to be a second chamber, we should take a closer look," he added.

"Yeah, okay," agreed Olivia.

They climbed and entered the next chamber, which was surrounded by four imposing statues of weather gods. Each one seemed to represent a force of nature. Behind them and on the back of the room was a large image, which was more colourful than the last. On it was a portrayal of a god kneeling down and from its hand came the same demons on ships.

In the centre, there were islanders attacking and preparing them for sacrifice. Next was a drawing of the demons being sacrificed for the gods, with blood being absorbed by another god.

"This seems to be exactly what happened earlier, and what they tried to do to you," Olivia pointed out as she took in what was on the display.

"It's as if they believe that any outsider that comes to the island is a challenge laid down by the gods they worship. They hunt down and sacrifice them, possibly to show they are worthy of the land they have?" said Thomas.

"That sounds likely. I imagine the traumatic attack from ships thousands of years ago, and the subsequent isolation has laid the foundations for this belief system to thrive."

"Then we are in serious danger. I imagine we are still being…what?" Callum paused, looking towards Lauren. She was standing petrified to the spot with a horrified expression on her face. Callum turned around and saw a group of islanders entering the temple.

"Quick hide," ordered Thomas.

The group took cover on the upper level of the shrine and could see the group of five islanders searching frantically below. They were armed with an assortment of long blades, bows and blunt weapons. Thomas gestured towards the back of the room at an exit. A wooden platform led towards the exit so they moved towards it slowly whilst crouched down.

Seemingly eager to escape, Callum went first. He was silent at first, but then he came across a crack in the ground without noticing it, and he fell a short distance to the lower floor as the wood gave way. The islanders yelled out as they saw him and began racing over.

"Damn it!" Thomas shouted.

"CALLUM!" Lauren cried out.

Seeing there was no way for Callum to climb back up as the drop was too great a distance, Thomas looked around and saw that there was another way up to the higher level through a passageway.

"Callum, go left! The path leads to a ledge where I can reach you!" advised Thomas, as he gestured towards the target area.

Callum had hurt his leg badly in the fall and began to move but very slowly. He reached the ledge in a few moments, but the islanders were hot on his tail due to his injury. Thomas lowered his hands to try and grab him.

"Come on, grab my hand!" Thomas shouted.

"I can't reach!" Callum desperately replied.

"Come on, dammit; you can do it!"

Lauren and Olivia reached the ledge and also started putting their arms down in a futile attempt to reach Callum. He turned around and saw the islanders' mere feet away. He made one last attempt at grabbing the hands reaching down for him, and then his expression faded of any hope as he looked Lauren in the eyes.

"I'm sorry," Callum said directly at Lauren.

As he uttered this, a blade cut through his body, and the islanders cut him down. Lauren screamed and in denial at what was happening tried to jump down and help, only to be pulled back by Olivia. She broke away from Olivia and grabbed the handgun that was in Thomas' holster. She began firing rapidly at the islanders and managed in the frantic hail of bullets to kill them all.

As the gun clicked indicating it had run out of bullets, she dropped it and slipped down to Callum. Upon reaching him, she immediately took an item of clothing and applied pressure to the wound. It was pouring blood, and she knew it was futile but was desperate to avoid the worst.

"Listen to me, listen to me, baby. We are going to get you wrapped up and out of here, you understand?" Lauren pleaded.

"Lauren. I…" Callum murmured.

He reached into his pocket and pulled out the ring. He grabbed her hand and placed it firmly inside.

"In Spain…at the Villa. I was going to ask you to marry me."

"What?"

"In Spain, I was going to ask you to marry me."

"Yes, (she briefly paused) Yes. My answer would be and is yes."

She put the ring on and grabbed him gently by the back of the head and pulled him in close.

"Things didn't quite work out hey?"

"Don't say that. We are getting you out of here."

Voices could be heard yelling from the front of the hall. More islanders had heard the gunshots and were coming to see what was going on.

"Olivia, please help? OLIVIA?" Lauren shouted, looking up at Thomas and Olivia, who were standing looking down. They knew the situation was futile. Lauren looked back at Callum.

"I love you," Callum said, looking at Lauren.

"I love you too."

Lauren gave him a gentle kiss and then embraced him in a final hug as the voices got louder and closer. She looked back at Callum who had passed away. His head sank into his chest in a silent bow.

"Callum. CALLUM?" Lauren cried out.

"Come on, grab my hand!" Thomas ordered, extending his hand in urgency.

Lauren began to cry, and her focus was solely on the lifeless body of Callum.

"Lauren!" Olivia shouted.

"Come on, time is running out, more are coming!" said Thomas.

The voices cut through, and she stood up and ran over to Thomas. She grabbed his hand and was pulled up just as the islanders came into view. The islanders arrived at the scene and appeared briefly distracted by their fallen. Olivia, Thomas and Lauren moved towards the exit and ran for it while the islanders were looking at the bodies amongst the mini massacre. Lauren stopped and turned to face the scene, as tears rolled down her cheeks.

"Lauren, we have got to go!" Olivia said, putting her hands on Lauren's face. "I am sorry. We have got to go, now!"

Lauren weakly nodded, and they ran and caught up with Thomas who was waiting at an exit, gesturing towards the way out. They headed down a small flight of steps and then began running as fast as they could, with no idea where they were heading other than away from the temple. After a few minutes of constant running, the energy drained from Olivia, and she knew everyone else was feeling it too. When she knew they were a safe distance from the temple, for now, she gestured to the others to stop.

"Okay, I think we have lost them for now," Thomas said, as he and Olivia turned to face Lauren, who as soon as she stopped running started to sob as if the only thing that had stopped the tears was the energy required to sprint away.

"Lauren, I'm so sorry," Olivia said as she embraced her in a close hug, while Lauren cried as the emotion of losing Callum couldn't be held in any longer.

"I can't believe he is dead," Lauren said in complete denial of what had just happened.

"I'm so sorry I brought you here."

"You couldn't have known."

Thomas came over and put his hand on her shoulder.

"I know the raw feeling of loss that you must have right now. I had it when Arthur died right in front of me all those years ago. But we have got to try and put all of this to one side for now so we can survive this hell," Thomas supportively added.

"He was a great friend, and we will mourn him," assured Olivia. "But now isn't the time. Thomas is right. We need to stay strong as best we can."

"Okay. You're right," acknowledged Lauren as she nodded, wiping away her tears and looking up. "What now?"

"I, I don't know. We should keep moving, try and find some shelter and figure something out," Thomas said, less confident than usual.

"Okay then," Lauren said before wandering ahead slightly aimless, the death of Callum still not seeming a complete reality. She got far enough away that she couldn't hear Olivia and Thomas.

"We need to keep close to her. What has just happened has shocked us all but not as much as Lauren. We need to make sure she gets through this as strong as she can," Thomas said, putting his hand on Olivia's shoulder reassuringly.

"She has a tough spirit within her, it has just been dimmed a little. I will keep her close."

They both smiled faintly and then began to move forward to catch up with Lauren.

Chapter Sixteen

"Wow, look at that!" Olivia exclaimed as she stopped in her tracks and stared up in wonder.

Thomas walked slightly in front of her and joined her in awe. Ahead of them was a very large structure, which looked more extravagant than anything else they had seen so far. It became obvious that as they went past the temple, they had entered the more central parts of the island that were seemingly reserved for the more elite members of its society.

"It's some kind of palace by the looks of it. I imagine back when this place was fully functioning this was the heart of the island," observed Thomas.

"Let's take a look. Besides it's clouding over, the shelter would be a good idea," Olivia recommended.

"Yeah, okay, that sounds great to me," said Lauren.

The front doorway was half-open, so Thomas took the lead and pushed the door. It was stiff and wouldn't budge at first, but after Olivia helped, it opened up, and what it was hiding was revealed.

"Incredible," exclaimed Olivia.

They were met with a spacious front hall with a large staircase in the centre, which led up to an old stone balcony that was crumbling away at its far edges. At the very top was an exposed doorway.

"Curious to take a look?" enquired Olivia with a smile.

"Oh absolutely, you read my mind," Thomas replied.

They carefully climbed the stairs and entered through the doorway. Beyond was a room full of royal looking décor and although the majority of the room was empty, at the back was a throne.

"This must be where the Queen ruled from," remarked Olivia.

"This place had a Queen?" asked Lauren.

"Yes, according to legend when the King discovered this island and added it to his empire, his Queen was presented this as a gift to rule over. The two couldn't bear to be apart, but the lure of her own island proved too much of a temptation for the Queen."

"And was she here when it was attacked?"

"I don't know. I would assume so by seeing this. I imagine from what we have seen of this island that there must have been a loss of power and control once the attack was over."

"I think she may have been here when that happened and still is. Take a look at this," Thomas added, who had found a small opening behind the throne that led to another chamber. Curiosity began to mix with a brief burst of excitement as they all followed Thomas in.

They all walked through and into a corridor that was around 15-20 metres in length. A total of ten large stone warriors with weapons drawn surrounded them, with five on each side evenly lining the pathway to the opening at the end.

"Incredible. Even after all of these years, the detail is magnificent," remarked Thomas.

"Do either of you know what they are?" asked Lauren.

"Well, if my assumption that this is leading to a burial chamber for the Queen is correct, then these are representations of all ten of the Queen's guard. Similar to Egyptian culture, death was seen as not the end of one's life, just the soul's time on this Earth. Death was the journey to the afterlife, and just like on Earth they believed their duty of protection was to the Queen in life and death and wherever she went."

"So what happened to the guard upon their ruler's death?"

"It is likely that once the given ruler died, the sworn guardians would sacrifice their earthly bodies to follow her into the next life, whatever they believed that to be. It is probable that their bodies were placed inside of these statues as a way of showing their dedication," Thomas responded.

Lauren shuddered slightly as they reached the end of the hallway and passed through the doorway and into the next chamber. Inside was a Sarcophagus, which was in the centre of the room. There was a section of the roof missing so the light was able to illuminate enough of the tomb to see.

"This room, it's almost identical to that of the tomb that your father and I found all those years ago. And this Sarcophagus is extremely detailed," said Thomas in awe.

"Although worn, it looked very royal in style," Olivia responded.

"With that in mind and the fact that this appears to be the Queen's royal palace, this must be where she was laid to rest."

"Fascinating. So it looks like the myths about this place really are true. The island really does exist, and it really was ruined thousands of years ago."

"You almost feel sorry for the islanders with regard to what happened, at least the original generation who experienced it."

"They don't have my sympathy with what they have become today," Lauren added, with a low level of anger in her voice.

"I imagine when the Queen died, the island was lost. Seeing the palace taken by the enemy must have been the final nail in the coffin. I just wonder what happened next," speculated Olivia.

"The myths all state that after this place was attacked, the majority of the invaders left. I assume that was to travel home to inform their rulers what had been found to add it to their own empire. However, it would appear they never found it again, hence the beginning of thousands of years of searching," Thomas replied.

"And we are the ones who came across it," said Olivia.

"I think that after the invaders left and help never came, the island fell into disarray. All order and influence from Sutanda would have faded, and the belief in the Gods we see statues of all over the island began to emerge. This place would have become self-contained and without a ruler who knows what happened in the years that followed, pure chaos for a while no doubt."

"Erm, guys? Sorry to interrupt but look at what I have just found," Lauren cut in.

"What is…?" Olivia started to respond, but her jaw dropped before she could finish.

"Oh my," exclaimed Thomas.

In the back part of the room slightly exposed in the dim light, they were met with some assorted treasures, mostly gold and still shining after all these years.

"It's the lost treasure of Arcanum, it actually exists!" Olivia excitedly said.

"Bloody hell, Arthur was right!" stated Thomas.

"It must have been put in here to be with the Queen in death, to maybe guard it or to take it with her to the afterlife," Olivia hypothesised.

All three of them began to look through what was stashed away in the tomb. Assorted items of jewellery, coins, statues and relics from the ancient empire were scattered around in various chests and all over the floor.

"This could make us famous!" said Lauren.

"Quite more than that Lauren, this could make us rich. These are ancient Sutandan relics that were thought long lost. They would make quite the addition to the collection at the British Museum. It would highlight so many of the missing pieces of the cultural jigsaw," Thomas replied with a large grin across his face.

"Only problem being, there is no way we can get this off the island. We don't even have a way off ourselves," Olivia said, which lowered the level of excitement back down.

"Yes, I guess you are right," agreed Thomas. "I dread to even consider a return trip to this place if we ever got away from here, but that would be the only way."

"At least we know that my father's search wasn't in vain and that he was right."

"Come on, we had better keep moving. They will be hot on our heels after what we did to the attackers back there," Thomas remarked.

As Olivia and Thomas walked out of the doorway, Lauren turned and took one last look at the treasure. She took a few coins in her hand and examined the surprising amount of detail engraved on them.

"Lauren? Are you coming?" Olivia could be heard saying from halfway down the staircase.

"Coming, I was just, erm, looking one last time at what is in here," Lauren quickly responded.

When she picked up the coins she spied a ring adorned with a large red diamond and unable to resist the urge she slipped it into her bag along with a few coins. She decided to bring one with her to show Olivia and Thomas so she didn't appear guilty. She walked down the stairs towards them and showed them the coin.

"We thought we would be leaving you here!" Thomas joked.

"Sorry, I was distracted by this. Look," she said handing the coin over to Thomas.

"The level of detail that is still clear on this coin fascinates me."

"That is cool. Looks like it would have been a small change in this culture, but if we get out of here, it might get you a fair bit more. Keep it on you for luck," he said, handing it back to her.

Chapter Seventeen

After walking for half an hour or so from the Queen's burial chamber, they came across and followed a river that had got wider as they progressed along with it with a bank alongside. They had come to a viewpoint on a slight hill that looked down upon what appeared to be a small village. Thomas looked through his binoculars at what is ahead.

"Look downstream, there is a village which seems to be where a lot of the islanders live," said Thomas as he passed the binoculars around the group. Lauren looked first, followed by Olivia.

"We don't seem to have a way around it, but I think this could be used to our advantage," he said.

"How so?" Olivia replied slightly puzzled.

"You see there? There is a small boat. This seems to be a fishing location, meaning we are closer to the sea. If we can sneak through the village and steal the boat, we could reach the sea quicker, as well as making distance from these savages. I think getting to the coast will be a good move as we could look for any other boats," explained Thomas.

"Sneak in? Are you mad? They have just killed Callum as well as other people we came here with, and you want to get closer to them when they don't know where we are!" said Lauren, clearly voicing opposition to the idea.

"Although they don't know where we are at the moment, they will find us. Unfortunately, that is a certainty. We don't know this place, but they do. We need to take advantage of this while we can and seize the element of surprise. Olivia, what do you think?" asked Thomas.

"As much as I don't want to be near them, I agree with you. If we are to get out of here, I think we need to take that boat. We can't go back the way we came and find our original lifeboat so it's the next best option. How are we going to go about it?"

"I think we should go to that entrance there by the rocks, using them as cover. Then we should move to the hut on the right and then split up into two groups. I will go along the more visible route and distract the islanders overlooking the boat, while you climb on a board. Once you are on, I will come over, and we can leave. Hopefully, they won't notice until we are already downstream," Thomas advised.

"That sounds crazy enough to work and does make sense. Okay, I'm in," agreed Lauren.

A few raindrops fell as the sky began to cloud over in a change of weather.

"It's starting to rain. This will work in our favour sneaking through," said Olivia as she looked up towards the sky.

"It's as if their weather gods are helping us," laughed Thomas.

With that, they all slowly made their way down the slope by the river and in a few minutes were within metres of the entrance to the village. The rain had become much heavier, something that Olivia was extremely grateful for.

"Okay, as planned. Ready?" asked Thomas quietly.

Olivia and Lauren nodded nervously. Thomas then gestured for them to move, and they went through the open wooden gate. They headed to the right and alongside a hut. Olivia carefully looked through a window, and this revealed two islanders going about general business inside.

Lauren knocked into a wind chime outside, which drew the attention of one of the islanders. He walked up to the window that they were crouched under. He looked out suspiciously, and his gaze just missed Lauren. He then got called by the other islander and headed back away from the window.

Feeling it was clear they carried on and reached the end of the cover the hut provided. They saw one islander standing looking towards the boat. Thomas gestured for Olivia and Lauren to move forward, and he moved along the small wooden bridge that went over the river. He moved behind a hut and threw a rock against a wall. This distracted the islander who moved away from the vantage point which gave Olivia and Lauren a window of opportunity.

Seeing it was safe to move forward, they both advanced towards the boat. They moved between two huts, and Olivia looked back towards Thomas. He was slowly moving down the bank towards them when Olivia saw an islander sneak up behind Thomas and take him down. He pulled him away with another islander.

Olivia was horrified and looked back towards Lauren, and she was also gone. Olivia suddenly became panicked, and she frantically looked around and stepped backwards trying to take in any clues in her surroundings. She moved her body around and then felt something grab her, and everything went black.

The next thing Olivia remembered was a brief and sharp pain in the face as she was slapped hard by a female islander. She came to and looked around, still desperate to locate Lauren. She saw her tied against a wooden beam in a hut, and as she tried to move, she felt her hands were behind her back and bound with a thin rope. The attacker screamed in her face and hit her once more before turning and heading towards Lauren.

She picked up a bag from a table which Olivia immediately recognised as Lauren's, and it was turned upside down and emptied all over the floor. The ring and few coins that Lauren had taken from the palace hit the floor and as the islander saw it she picked up the ring and yelled at Lauren in a rage. The ring was recognised and seemed to have some importance to her, and she struck her once more. She grabbed a large wooden bat that was against a wall and moved to hit Lauren with it, whose eyes were full of fear and with tears running down her cheeks.

As the wood was raised and about to be swung, a large male walked into the room and stopped her, ushering her outside. She dropped the bat on the floor and immediately left the room, with the door closing behind her.

"Lauren, are you okay?" Olivia asked.

"As okay as I can be tied to a pole in a savages hut on an island that no one knows exists. I'm fantastic," Lauren sarcastically replied.

"They've gone. We need to find a way out of here before they come back, look around!"

"Where is Thomas?"

"Just before they took me, I remember seeing him get grabbed as we did. He is probably in another hut nearby. We need to get out and find him."

"Olivia, your gun is over there."

Olivia looked and saw the gun, and her belongings were just out of reaching distance. Her knife, however, was a little closer.

"My knife is closest. If I can just reach it I may be able to cut us loose."

"Look, to your left. That woman dropped a wooden bat. Can you reach it?"

"I think so."

Olivia stretched her leg as far as it could go to the left and managed to slowly move the bat towards her. She put the bat between both legs and then used it to roll the knife towards them. She grabbed it with her fingers and then began cutting at the rope. It broke, and she then gave it to Lauren.

As she did, the female islander came back in and saw what was going on. She lunged towards Olivia, and the two began to fight. Olivia got knocked to the ground, and the islander picked up the bat and went to hit Lauren, who was still struggling to free herself. Olivia attempted to grab the islander from behind but was thrown back to the floor.

She looked up and saw her handgun. She knew firing it would attract attention, but she didn't see any other option. She fired two shots at the islander who dropped the bat and turned towards Olivia. She lunged at her as Olivia fired one final shot that killed the enraged islander.

As they dropped to the floor, Olivia and Lauren could hear multiple voices outside that had begun to shout and yell. They knew something was wrong, and Olivia had little time. She freed Lauren, and they left immediately through the front.

"THOMAS! THOMAS, WHERE ARE YOU?" shouted Olivia.

Olivia and Lauren began moving about almost aimlessly while awaiting a response. It wasn't long until she got one as she heard Thomas scream out a few times. They listened intently and zoned in on where he was. Olivia and Lauren moved towards the sound and arrived at a hut that was almost identical to the one they were held in. Olivia kicked open the door and moved in. They saw Thomas tied up against a wooden pole with two islanders attacking him.

As they entered, Olivia fired two shots at the nearest islander. He fell in seconds, and she then aimed at the second who turned to face her at the sound of the shots. She pulled the trigger, but it clicks indicating it was empty.

"Shit!" Olivia muttered.

The islander confronted Olivia, pushing her back against the wall. Knowing she was too weak to help, Lauren ran to Thomas and immediately began cutting him loose. Olivia struggled to fend off the attacker, and as she looked to be in a bad way, Thomas grabbed him from behind and took him down.

"Thanks, but we aren't out of trouble just yet. Sounds as if they know we are here. We need to get to that boat, now!" Thomas said.

They all headed for the door and went immediately towards the boat. Surprisingly the area around it was unguarded, and all the screaming voices were approaching from behind with increasing menace. As they reached the boat, they could see that it was secured to a nearby wooden beam by a thick rope.

"I'm going to need a minute to cut this loose," Thomas advised.

"We don't have a minute, we need to go!" Lauren shouted over to Thomas.

"I haven't got any ammo left in my handgun; how are we supposed to hold them off?" Olivia asked. Thomas threw a handgun magazine over, and she caught it and slammed it into her gun.

"It's my last one. Keep them back and make every shot count!"

At the end of the wooden walkway, several villagers had arrived, some with assorted weapons. They began slowly advancing on them as Olivia aimed her gun and fired a warning shot in the air. Most of them were startled and dropped back, but two carried on moving forward. One was armed, and the other was not.

"I haven't got enough to hold them all off!"

"Almost there, just a little longer!"

One of them began to charge at Olivia, and by the time, she opened fire and took him down the other armed with a long knife attacked. By the time she pulled the trigger, he was within close range. A small discharge of blood hit her chest and arm as the attacker slumped to the ground. The screaming of the crowd intensified as more arrived.

"Okay done, get on quick!"

They all got on, and Thomas grabbed the oars and started rowing. They pulled away and realised they were on a downstream flow, as the small boat picked up speed quickly. Slightly relieved, Lauren looked towards Olivia and noticed her face drop. Lauren turned and saw that they were being followed downstream by an almost identical boat with three islanders.

One had a bow and arrow, and the other had a few throwing knives. Olivia turned and fired the last few remaining handgun shots, but only a few hit the underside of the pursuing boat. A few arrows nearly hit them as they began to pick up speed. The river took a few bends and then began to narrow drastically. Olivia, out of ideas, noticed a bow underneath the rear seat of the boat and fired a wild arrow which missed.

"Hang tight!" Thomas yelled out.

The boat followed the river around a sharp turn, and Olivia was knocked over. Upon sitting up she saw that the islanders were now very close. A few knives were thrown and impacted the side of the boat, one penetrating the wood and half sticking through. Olivia fired one more bow at the islander rowing the pursuing boat and hit them.

Just after this, the islanders hit a large rock within the river, and the boat broke apart. Olivia felt a slightly smug look across her face, but this was short-lived. She turned to tell Thomas but saw they were at the top of a waterfall.

"Hold on to something!" shouted Thomas.

The boat began to descend down a steep section of the river before falling down a waterfall. It wasn't very high so it didn't break the boat on impact. However, as they landed and got propelled forward by the current, Olivia turned to see Lauren had fallen overboard.

"LAUREN! Stop the boat, Lauren has fallen overboard!" she screamed at Thomas.

Thomas positioned the boat to be against the current as they both scoured the water for any sign of Lauren. She soon popped out of the foam at the bottom of the fall but was struggling against the current.

"Hold us steady," Thomas said as he handed the oars to Olivia and jumped into the water and swam over to Lauren, helping bring her back towards the boat. As Olivia helped them aboard, the islanders could be heard just beyond the top of the waterfall.

"We need to move," Olivia exclaimed, her gaze focused on the top of the waterfall as shadows of islanders began to appear one by one. Thomas looked up and nodded and checked on Lauren who was shaken but unhurt. Thomas resumed moving the boat down the river, and it was soon apparent they had made it to where the river met the sea. In front of them, something large emerged, and as it crept into view, Olivia felt a fresh wave of dread.

Chapter Eighteen

The large unknown structure slowly came into view and a sinking feeling in Olivia's gut grew more intense. As they got closer alongside the object, it became obvious it was not an immediate threat, and it was the ship that was told of in the diary she had read earlier.

"What's that?" asked Lauren.

"It's a large shipwreck. It doesn't look like it has been here many years either, in relative to the environment at least," observed Thomas.

"It must be the ship that the crew mentioned in the diary came from. I think we should investigate, see if we can find out more clues as to what happened," said Olivia.

"Okay, sounds a good idea to me," agreed Thomas.

Thomas manoeuvred the boat up alongside it, and they saw that this was a ship that had run aground on the island. The stern of the ship was still in the water, but the front half was stuck deep in the ground.

"Look, there is a lifeboat hanging over the edge of the rear deck. It doesn't appear to have been used," said Olivia, pointing up towards the deck.

"You are right. We should try and get up there and take a look. It will get us out of sight of those islanders as well, which could be a chance to rest up. I will take us beside it."

Thomas moved the boat closer along the side of the ship, as they looked for a way in. A hatch was slightly open, so they moved over, and Thomas pulled it open. He stepped onto the shipwreck, tied a rope between both the little boat and a hook on the inside of the steel door, and then helped Olivia and Lauren on board.

He then closed the door behind them, a slam of steel that echoed through the hallway. It was pitch black, so Olivia started moving her hands to her torch but was beaten by Thomas. Both lit them up and aimed it around to get their bearings.

"Hmm. Surprised this thing is still working," commented Thomas.

"We should try and get up to a higher deck so we can see better and find out if there is anything on board," said Olivia.

"Okay, good idea. Follow me."

They all slowly moved along the hallway and then came to a stairwell. The hall carried on ahead of them, but the stairs had more light coming from above.

"We should take the stairs, seems logical," advised Lauren.

All nodded in agreement and headed up the stairs, slowly and cautiously. They turned right at the top of the stairs and went through another door. This led into a large kitchen area, showing that this ship would have usually contained a large crew. Items were strewn all over, but there were no signs of any bodies or of a violent struggle. Moving on through they passed another hallway and entered a small room where they noticed a sign stating 'Radio Room'. The room was dimly lit through a dirty porthole, so the room was visible without reliance on torchlight.

"Look, there's a radio system," pointed Olivia as she went over to it to have a look.

"I can't imagine it is working? Although, none of the crew seems to be here…" said Thomas.

Thomas walked over to the machine and took a look, but it was painfully apparent there was no power.

"Damn. There isn't any power. And by the dust in here and the look of it, it's been out for a very long time," observed Thomas.

Olivia looked on the desk and saw a log that had an incomplete entry. She began reading over the last few pages while the others looked around. Lauren slowly walked into the far corner of the room and looked slightly horrified.

"Erm, guys?" she said.

"What is it?" asked Thomas.

Olivia and Thomas hurried over and saw what Lauren was looking to be two skeletal remains of crew members. They were identifiable by their still relatively intact uniforms. One of the skulls had its jaw open and had a look of terror ingrained upon it even in death. In its hand was a handgun that was empty. The second set of remains had something potentially much more important, a satellite phone.

"That log over there. It said that they were shrouded in strong fog one dark night, and they crashed here and ran aground. It doesn't mention anything about any danger other than they were going to try and look for help," commented Olivia.

"And it looks as if the islanders got them?" said Thomas.

186

"This is all eerily similar to what I saw on our ship before it sank. Those depictions we saw in the tomb of the gods offering up souls to be sacrificed, it's happened here as well."

"Are these the same uniforms of the bodies you saw in that cave earlier on?"

Olivia nodded in agreement and as she crouched and took a closer look.

"They are yes. These poor people must have gone through the same experience that we are."

"Then we need to make sure we don't end up like them and keep focused," Thomas said, as he picked up the satellite phone and looked at it. Its battery had been removed so he walked over to the half-open cupboard next to the radio and checked for batteries. By chance, there was one next to the casing for what was presumably for the phone. He clicked it in place, and it came on.

"What was the frequency you tried earlier Olivia?" Thomas asked, fiddling around with the frequencies.

"I think it was the standard SOS frequency. Try that."

Thomas typed this into the phone and started a call.

"Hello, can anyone read me?" he asked, but there was nothing but silence.

"Say again, this is Thomas Moyes. I am shipwrecked and need an urgent response. Say again, I am shipwrecked with two others and need urgent assistance," but there was still no response, or even evidence it was functioning properly.

"I needed to reach higher ground before I could make contact. Let's try and make our way to the top deck and give it another shot," Olivia suggested.

"Good idea. And that way we can check and see if we can launch that lifeboat and get away from here."

"That gun, do you think there are more on board?" asked Lauren.

"I don't know, but we could do with some if there are, we are completely out of ammo," Olivia responded.

They left the room and moved into a stairwell that took them up to the bridge. Upon entering they walked forward towards the main ship controls. A body of who was presumed to be the Captain was collapsed by a desk with another logbook and various documents.

"Looks like the Captain. He has similar arrows in his body like we had fired at us," Olivia said as she looked over the slumped body.

"I think they had a very similar experience arriving here to what we had, poor souls," Thomas said, slightly disheartened.

"Look at this logbook. It has the last recorded location of this ship. If we get hold of SART, this could help them find us," said Olivia.

"Hopefully. It says their equipment gave out just before they ran aground, so it shouldn't be far off. I imagine it's in the direction they came from just out to sea. Right, I'm going to take a look at the lifeboat and see if it's seaworthy and alright to launch. It may be a good idea for you to have a look around and see if there is anything we can use."

"Okay," responded Olivia, as she gave Thomas a nod.

Thomas left the room, and Olivia and Lauren began looking around. Olivia came across a small map of the ship detailing the rooms aboard. Reading through she came across 'Armoury'. She started to wonder what kind of ship this was. Thomas then re-entered.

"It looks good. It's tied on by ropes, and as there isn't any power, I would need to lower us down manually and then cut the rope. But it's good news as it is undamaged, unlike our other little boat. Did you find anything?" asked Thomas.

"Look, there are various cabins and crew quarters that were uneventful, but then I read this," remarked Olivia.

"They have a weapon room?" Thomas replied with a surprised tone.

He then noticed the light on the satellite phone had gone green indicating a signal. With a burst of hope, he tried again to contact help.

"Hello, can anyone read me?" he again said into the phone with no response.

"Say again, this is Thomas Moyes. I am shipwrecked and need an urgent response. Say again, I am shipwrecked with two others and need urgent assistance."

A short time passed, and then the voice Olivia recognised from earlier came through on the phone.

"We hear you. Is this the same incident from a few hours ago?"

"Yes. I am here with Olivia King and Lauren Winters. We are shipwrecked in the South Pacific Ocean and need urgent assistance."

"We started a trace of your signal when the line cut off earlier but have not been able to get a location. Do you have any details?"

"The log!" said Olivia, who turned and went to get it, bringing it back over pointing to the coordinates that were written down.

"Last known coordinates are 200 miles south-west of Hanga Roa in the South Pacific Ocean," Thomas informed the man on the phone.

"That's coming up as one pretty isolated place, what are you doing there?"

"We were looking for something, and it kind of found us."

"Right, okay. Well, we are on our way to your location now. Keep this phone on you, as we will need to contact you again when we are nearby to locate you."

"Thank you—we will do. Over and out."

"Someone is coming?" Lauren excitedly asked.

"It would appear so, yes. I think we should get the lifeboat launched and head out to sea in the direction this ship has come from. That way, we are going to be away from this place and hopefully out of danger while we wait."

"Good idea," agreed Olivia.

"We need a sharp blade of some kind to cut the ropes on the lifeboat. Shall we go and have a look in the kitchen area we passed?" Thomas suggested.

"Sure, and if that fails, we can have a look in the armoury which is directly below it on the map," Olivia said.

With that, they headed back and went into the same darkened kitchen from a moment ago. There were a few windows on the portside wall, but it was quite dim. Thomas walked past a few more skeletal remains and came to a large cupboard door. He opened it and found a collection of knives ranging from small right up to cleavers. He picked up the largest one and turned to Olivia and Lauren.

"This could be ideal, we should…"

A loud thud interrupted him talking, and they all fell dead quiet. The sound came from down the stairs at the end of the hallway.

"Stay here and well hidden. I'll go and check it out," said Thomas.

He cautiously went down the stairs that led to the hallway in which they came aboard. The hatch through which they entered was slightly open and banging slightly against the hinges. Someone or something had opened it. He walked over to it and looked through the gap.

To his horror, he could see numerous islanders making their way towards the shipwreck. For a split second, he wondered how they knew where they were, then he realised that he tied the boat they stole from the village against the side of the ship. Thomas shut the door, and the hallway fell dark again. He clicked on the torch and began heading back.

Thomas reached the area with the stairwell, and he heard a slight movement behind him. He turned, and a dark shadowy figure emerged from the darkness and attacked him. The torch was knocked to the ground, and the only light was from the stairwell.

During the fight, Thomas was soon knocked down, and the figure began to strangle him, pinning him down. Thomas managed to wrestle an arm free and punched the figure who slightly lost grip. It was here that Thomas grabbed the cleaver and stabbed the figure repeatedly until he let go. The figure slumped to the ground with blood everywhere.

"Thomas!" called Olivia, who had arrived at the top of the stairs and rushed down immediately to assist. Lauren appeared as Olivia ran down.

"Are you okay? What happened?"

"I'm fine. But they know. They know we are here. We need to get that lifeboat launched and get out of here now!"

"Are there more of them?" asked Olivia.

"Yes. That one got in through the hatch we did, and when I closed it I saw them. They are all coming," warned Thomas.

"We need something to defend ourselves with, we should check that armoury. It's just down the hall."

She helped him up, and they moved further down the hall and into the armoury.

The room was quite small but full of gun racks on the walls. The majority of the room was empty, and it looked as if the crew of the ship ransacked it in desperation years before. However, there were a few weapons remaining and another body on the floor with a weapon still clutched in its bony grasp.

"Quickly, grab what you can and what you can use," ordered Thomas.

"I don't have any experience with a gun," Lauren said, slightly concerned.

"We can show you don't worry. I have only had a few sessions of clay pigeon shooting and days down the shooting range, but it's simple enough to pick up," Olivia said as she tried to reassure Lauren. Thomas then gave Lauren a handgun.

"First of all, this is the safety when you want to fire, click this into the upright position. Then aim towards your target and pull the trigger. Now, this one hasn't got much of a kick so you should be able to handle it but take your time between shots," he explained.

"Okay."

"Now you get fifteen bullets per magazine. When you run out, press this button on the side, and the magazine will drop out from here. To reload, take another magazine and slam it here. Then you are ready to continue firing."

"Okay, I think I've got it," said Lauren nervously.

"You will be fine. Hopefully, we can get out of this without you needing to shoot at anything," Olivia added, as she grabbed her on the shoulder briefly for reassurance.

"But just in case, we should be prepared," said Thomas, handing Olivia an assault rifle and replacement handgun, along with two magazines for each.

"Okay, let's get back up on deck and get out of here," said Olivia confidently.

As they began moving along the hallway that led to the stairwell the hatch door was opened quickly, and two islanders boarded. They yelled towards Olivia and the others and began running towards them. Thomas drew his handgun and fired a few shots taking them down. As he did so, more figures could be seen about to board.

"Come on, up the stairs!" ordered Thomas.

They ran up the stairs, through the kitchen and back up onto the top deck. Thomas uncovered the top of the lifeboat and ushered Olivia and Lauren on. He then began to operate the lowering system, and it began to slowly drop down.

"Wait, what about you?" enquired Olivia.

"I need to stay here and operate this so the boat lowers," Thomas replied.

"But how are you going to get on?"

"I will slide down the rope or throw down this emergency ladder, don't worry!"

"Be careful!"

Thomas then began turning the crank to lower the boat, and it picked up speed. Soon, Olivia and Lauren lost sight of the top deck as they descended down. As they reached halfway, the boat stopped moving down, and gunfire could be heard from the top deck.

"THOMAS!" shouted Olivia, with a gut wrench of nerves.

More gunfire was heard from above when suddenly islanders began attacking Olivia and Lauren through the deck windows they were hovering by. Olivia started firing her assault rifle in controlled bursts as the islanders carried on firing bows and throwing sharp objects. They fended off this group of attackers, and as they did, Thomas looked over to confirm they were okay.

Olivia was happy to see he appeared to be alright and gave a thumbs up. The boat continued to lower and got within a metre or so from the sea when it stopped. Due to the shipwrecks position, the rope wasn't quite long enough.

"That's all the rope we have!" Thomas shouted down.

Thomas fired another full magazine of his assault rifle as the islanders began to greatly outnumber him on the top deck. With the gun now empty, he put the weapon over his back and climbed onto the rope. He began to slide down as more islanders began attacking the now hanging lifeboat, with Olivia and Lauren returning fire covering Thomas as he descended.

As soon as he landed on the boat he immediately began cutting the rope. He handed Olivia a second knife that he had picked up and gestured she do the same.

"We need to cut these both at the same time so we land evenly," he advised Olivia.

"Okay, on your mark," she replied.

"Three, two, one, now!" Thomas shouted.

They both frantically cut at the rope, and it broke. The boat dropped the metre or so it was hanging above the water and landed slightly unevenly front first, which knocked everyone over. Thomas then grabbed the oars and started to move the ship away from the wreck as fast as he could.

"Cover us!" Thomas shouted.

Olivia and Lauren both began firing controlled bursts of assault rifle bullets into the attackers as they slowly pulled away. Lauren ran out of ammo first and turned towards Olivia for more.

"Olivia, I need more..." said Lauren, but she stopped mid-sentence.

Suddenly an arrow penetrated her torso, and she looked down in shock. Lauren dropped her weapon and grabbed the arrow with one hand, and a moment after she realised what had happened, she collapsed. Olivia was hit with a sharp feeling of disbelief and shock before looking up and seeing the individual who fired the arrow.

Any feeling she had was immediately overtaken by rage, and she took aim and fired at the man on the pursuing boat, taking him out with surprising ease. The boat stopped and a chorus of shouts from the islanders who were now out of attacking range amped up as they saw who appeared to be in charge taken down.

Olivia threw her gun down and checked on Lauren. She was bleeding from her side and was looking up.

"Lauren! Lauren, look at me, you are going to be okay. Just stay with me!"

Lauren moved her mouth a few times in an attempt to talk, but then her head tilted to one side, and her eyes closed.

Olivia's heart sank as she felt her friend slipping away in her arms.

"Check her pulse!" Thomas shouted, who was still frantically moving the boat as far away as possible from the islanders.

Olivia placed her hand on Lauren's neck and felt a faint pulse, confirming she had just passed out.

"Anything?" asked Thomas.

"Yes, yes. There is a pulse, it's faint, but she is still alive."

"I imagine she has passed out from the shock, stay with her. I am going to get us as far as away as I can before stopping."

"Okay."

Olivia kept her arm on Lauren as they moved away, checking her temperature and heart rate often. Olivia looked motionlessly at the shipwreck and the surrounding coastline as it drifted further and further away until she could not see it anymore. Not long after this, the energy completely drained from her body, and she fell asleep.

Chapter Nineteen

"Olivia. Olivia!" Thomas repeated as he tried to wake her. Olivia slowly opened her eyes to see Thomas briefly shaking her.

"Look, over there!" he said, with a little excitement in his voice.

Less than 25 metres or so ahead a large rescue boat was coming up towards them. It was a SART vessel. Olivia stood, and a large rush of emotions hit her, a large mixture of relief and happiness but also sadness that the others couldn't be there with them.

"They found us!"

"That they did," Thomas replied, looking at her with a faint smile. She hugged him.

The boat slowly came up alongside them, and they were brought up onto the deck by a crew member. He immediately gave them a bottle of water each, which Olivia and Thomas drank.

"Thank you. Thank you so much," said Olivia.

"No problem. Is this everyone?" the crew member asked.

"Yes, please can you help my friend? She was wounded on the way here, and she has been unconscious ever since. She is still bleeding."

"Of course," he confirmed, waving over to some colleagues of his. "Hey, we need medical assistance immediately!"

A man and woman hastily ran across the deck and carefully picked up Lauren and carried her off into the ship interior.

"Where are they taking her?" Olivia asked.

"We have an excellent medical team on board who will do everything they can. I think it would be wise to get you checked over as well, follow me."

"Okay, thank you."

They followed the man through the same door Lauren had just been taken through and walked along some hallways and into a medical room. There were three beds, and the one on their right had the curtain half pulled around it. Olivia saw it was Lauren, and there were three doctors working on her wound. One looked up at her and closed the curtain immediately.

"Please don't worry, they are excellent at what they do, and they are her best chance at getting through it. Best leave them to it. Please come here, the both of you. I want to check your vitals and see if you are okay," a female doctor said, trying her best to reassure Olivia.

Olivia sat on the bed, and the doctor began various tests. She was asked to lay down, and she did so, and although it wasn't the softest bed to lay back on, compared to the rocky ground on the island, it was luxurious. Her mind began to wander, and she didn't take notice of what the doctor was doing for a few moments. She was in a state of shock and still processing everything that happened.

To Olivia's amazement, other than a few cuts and bruises she had managed to escape relatively unscathed, with the same going to Thomas.

"…and your blood pressure is normal. I am glad to say that other than being dehydrated you are doing okay," the doctor said as she smiled at Olivia.

There was a knock at the door, and the same crew member from earlier walked in.

"I am glad to see Doctor Monroe is taking good care of you."

"She is. Thank you again for coming to rescue us."

"Oh, not at all. Please let me show you to your room. We want you to get as rested as soon as possible, after which the captain and the rest of the crew, myself included, want to know what happened to you if that is okay," the crew member asked.

"Of course that is fine. It is the least we can do," Olivia replied.

After a few minutes and an okay from the doctor, they walked through the ship, and Olivia was shown to a fairly large room.

"Unfortunately the only clothes we have for you in what appears to be your size are from our doctor's wardrobe, but there are shower facilities, and you can get some sleep here. We are going to get you home, but as you know this place is quite far from anywhere, you could call home so it will be a little while yet."

"Thank you."

"No problem. The change of clothes is on the bed, I do hope it is okay. Come and find us when you are ready to talk, but please take as long as you need to rest," he said, turning and heading back down the hall.

Olivia closed the door and entered the room. She walked over to the mirror and looked closely at her face in the reflection. She saw her face was slightly off colour, with the mix of blood and dirt that she had endured still faintly present, seemingly painted onto her pores. Her blue eyes slightly welled up in emotion, stared out from her drained face as her brown hair wildly hung down.

She looked as exhausted as she felt, as recent events had taken it out of her. She went straight to the shower and started to wash, and as she did she looked down and stood completely still, the water rushing through her hair. In this moment of reflection, she found herself still getting her head around everything that had just happened.

Sharp flashes of all of the events that had just unfolded come to the top of her mind, and they were as visceral as well as raw as they were earlier on. After the shower, she dried off and collapsed straight onto the bed, and within a few moments, she fell into a deep and much-needed sleep.

A knock at the door a few hours later woke her, and she opened the door to be greeted by Doctor Monroe.

"I hope you don't mind me disturbing you."

"No, not at all."

"Your friend, she is awake and asking for you."

"She is awake?"

"Yes, we have removed the object that was stuck in her torso and have closed the wound. I am cautiously optimistic that she is going to make a complete recovery over time. Please, come with me."

"That is so good to hear, thank you so much. Okay, let's go."

Going back along the hall, Olivia followed the doctor into the medical room, and she gestured towards Lauren. Walking in, she saw Lauren sat up at a slight angle in the bed. She looked a little shaken and drained, but she looked up and gave Olivia a warm smile.

"You had us worried back there, you know," Olivia said, smiling back.

"How did we get here?" Lauren asked.

"I am not sure how long it was until we were found as I blacked out, but a SART ship heard the distress call that we made on that shipwreck and were on their way to the area. When we drifted away from the island, we crossed paths, and they picked us up. I was so happy they found us, especially as you were badly injured."

"They are taking good care of me. I don't remember much of what happened, it's a bit of a blur, but I know an arrow or something pierced my side. I thought I was a goner you know."

"Not on my watch, not a chance."

A faint knock was heard at the door, and they all turned to see Thomas standing in the doorway.

"How are you holding up?" he asked.

"Okay, thank you, and how about yourself?"

"Yeah, I am doing alright, slowly recovering. A little sleep has done me well. And more importantly, how are you Lauren?" said Thomas.

"Getting there, I was just saying to Olivia it is just surreal how we have been rescued and are safe again."

"I know, it was perfect timing when they found us, I am not sure how much longer you could have gone without medical attention. You are very lucky indeed, and I am grateful for that."

"Well, I think that as the wound has been stitched up and treated, a lot of rest will do the world of good," said Doctor Monroe, which Olivia and Thomas picked up as a friendly hint to leave so they could carry on her recovery.

"They are ready for us in the briefing room by the way, if you are ready of course," added Thomas.

"Yeah, sure, have they been waiting long? I fell asleep and have lost track on time."

"I have been chatting to them for a little while to keep them entertained, but they want to hear from you. I have built you up as a bit of a key speaker," he said, trying to make her smile a little.

"Okay, lead the way old man," she said with a smile as she looked back at Lauren.

They walked through the ship and into the briefing room. There were ten crew members present, and the captain walked over and shook Olivia's hand. She then stood at the front of the room, and after locking eyes with Thomas, she smiled and then began to tell the story of everything that happened from the moment she found the secret room up until that moment.

She told it all, except that they found the treasure. She felt that if people find out it was there, that more people will risk their lives in trying to claim it as their own. In her mind, enough blood had been shed.

After the discussion with the crew, a few hours had passed, and it was evening. Olivia walked out onto the rear deck and sat with Thomas on a bench facing the ocean. They had recently had a full meal and were starting to feel more normal than they had over the last day or so.

"We found it," said Thomas.

"But at what cost? All those lives lost, all at my idea to find that place," Olivia replied.

"They all died with adventure in their hearts and the desire of discovery in their veins. If it was you, your father or someone else, the same thing would have happened. You saw the other bodies and the ship we were on back there. Other people suffered the same fate, but we got out. Question is, do we tell the world what really happened, about the existence of that place?"

"I want to warn people, but I believe that if we tell the world it's there, more people will go there, and more death will come. That is why I held back telling the crew of this ship about the fact that we did find the treasure."

"Then we keep it a mystery. We keep our tales of that island locked up (touching his chest) in here."

Olivia smiled faintly and touched his shoulder. She stood and began to walk towards the far railing on the deck.

"What are you going to do now?" asked Thomas.

"I'm going to take some time, and let all of what has happened sink in. Then I'm going to see what other mysteries are hidden amongst us, what stones have been left unturned by humanity."

"You are starting to sound more and more like your father every day, you know that?"

"I'm going to make him proud," Olivia said, smiling.

"You already do, and I think you know that."

She smiled before turning and watching as the setting sun reflected off the ripples of the sea, and the ship moved through the water heading home. She reached into her pocket and pulled out a small amulet on a string that she had taken from the treasure they had discovered. She placed it around her neck and decided this trinket would be a reminder of everything that had happened, including her father's sacrifice.

Olivia knew deep down in her heart, even after everything that had happened, that her father's urge for discovery had surfaced within her. Feeling it pulse within her body, she knew that an adventurer had been born. The question now was where would it take her next? She for one could not wait.